"I shouldn't be dancing with you,"

Margo murmured. "You're the enemy."

"I don't have to be," Kurt said. He guided her gently across the floor, closer to the band.

"Don't think that because I'm letting you dance with me, I'll give in to you about the store. I won't."

"No?" An amused twinkle was back in his eyes.

"No," she replied matter-of-factly. "Although you *are* the handsomest enemy I've ever done a two-step with...."

"I tango, too," he offered.

"Doesn't make any difference."

"I think it does." Kurt's dark eyes seemed to bore into Margo's soul, arousing emotions she'd forced herself to hold in check. "Something's happening between us," he said, his voice suddenly husky. "And it's going to be difficult to stay on opposite sides of the fence."

Dear Reader:

The spirit of the Silhouette Romance Homecoming Celebration lives on as each month we bring you six books by continuing stars!

And we have a galaxy of stars planned for 1988. In the coming months, we're publishing romances by many of your favorite authors such as Annette Broadrick, Sondra Stanford and Brittany Young. Beginning in January, Debbie Macomber has written a trilogy designed to cure any midwinter blues. And that's not all—during the summer, Diana Palmer presents her most engaging heroes and heroines in a trilogy that will be sure to capture your heart.

Your response to these authors and other authors of Silhouette Romances has served as a touchstone for us, and we're pleased to bring you more books with Silhouette's distinctive medley of charm, wit and—above all—romance.

I hope you enjoy this book and the many stories to come. Come home to romance—for always!

Sincerely,

Tara Hughes
Senior Editor
Silhouette Books

COLLEEN CHRISTIE

A Kiss is Still a Kiss

Silhouette *Romance*

Published by Silhouette Books New York

America's Publisher of Contemporary Romance

To CAM.
And Thanks To
MAR and HVM.

SILHOUETTE BOOKS
300 E. 42nd St., New York, N.Y. 10017

Copyright © 1988 by J.S. Bidwell

ISBN: 0-373-08558-3

First Silhouette Books printing February 1988

America's Publisher of Contemporary Romance

Printed in the U.S.A.

COLLEEN CHRISTIE

loves to travel and has seen most of Europe, though Hawaii remains her favorite spot. This new romance writer is an amateur thespian, a history buff, a trivia maniac and a "videophile" with an enormous collection of movie musicals. Colleen also collects motion picture soundtracks, which she uses as background music to write by. Her important literary influences range from Agatha Christie and Colleen McCullough to Erma Bombeck.

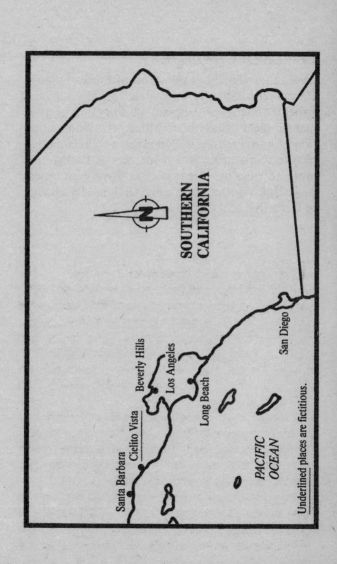

SOUTHERN CALIFORNIA

Santa Barbara
Cielito Vista
Beverly Hills
Los Angeles
Long Beach
San Diego

PACIFIC OCEAN

Underlined places are fictitious.

Chapter One

There was no doubt about it: he'd seen her.

Wildly, Margo Shepard looked around the Este-ridge Tower Hotel's banquet hall. She'd had it with David Cort and his constant proposals of marriage. She had tried reasoning with her ex-fiancé and avoid-ing him, but now she decided to shock him back to reality. Maybe some sort of blatant display of indif-ference to his affections would finally penetrate his granite skull.

Rows of chairs covered in burgundy velvet stretched in all directions in the large room, but only about half of them were occupied. The other video store owners were settling down in the lecture halls for the next seminar on selling prerecorded videocassettes.

But videocassettes could wait. Margo wouldn't be able to pay attention anyway. It had been difficult concentrating on the lectures the past day or so; Da-vid had a disconcerting habit of turning up at any moment, and invariably the matrimonial cat-and-mouse game would begin again. Well, she thought, it's time for this mouse to show a certain cat—once and for all—that she's *not* interested.

She made a sharp right turn, squeezing between two especially wide male merchants. A scattering of men and women clustered around the table behind the two men, perusing their seminar notebooks and joking with one another.

One man, seated a little to the side, didn't seem to be part of the between-lectures banter. In fact, he looked bored and wasn't bothering to hide it. He glanced up at Margo as she approached. Sudden interest flickered in his deep brown eyes, and an even smile creased his clean, strong features. He leaned back to get a better look at her, closing his notebook as he did so and scooping it from his lap. The look he gave her was boldly evaluating—and he seemed to like what he saw.

Unnerved, Margo dropped her gaze, looking down at her feet as she tried to pick her way around his long legs, which were partially blocking the aisle. With her eyes still down, she smacked directly into the back of another retailer as he rose from his seat, and the impact made her stagger. For a moment Margo thought she would regain her balance, but the man she'd run into turned toward her suddenly, knocking her farther backward. Her legs shot out from under her, and she fell with a thump—directly into the lap of the unsettling stranger.

At least he was a pretty solid cushion for her fall. She could feel his strong thighs beneath her as she teetered in his lap, and he steadied her by slipping a wide, warm hand around her waist as naturally as if it belonged there. Her skin prickled with excitement at the touch, and she felt a flush of embarrassment flood her cheeks as he pressed her against his muscular chest.

"Do me a favor," she demanded in a hoarse whisper.

He smiled even wider, showing fine white teeth. "Anything you say."

Margo swallowed. She'd never intended to go this far to discourage David, but desperate measures were called for: she threw her arms around his neck.

"Act like you know me—real well!" Margo gave him a convincing hug. This demonstration, she thought, should give David the shock he needed to get her message.

The handsome stranger complied eagerly, enfolding her in his strong arms. She hadn't expected such enthusiastic participation. In fact, he seemed to be entering into his impromptu role in her deception with great relish, she thought shakily as his grip tightened, and her pulse began to race.

Then, without warning, his lips captured hers with frightening passion, and she tried to cry out—but somehow the only sound that escaped her was a sort of muffled moan as her senses exploded like overloaded electrical wires. He pulled back slightly, hot breath against her cheek fanning an instant bonfire within her before his lips closed over hers again. She shuddered in surprise at the aching feeling deep inside her. Whose idea was this, anyway? Her arms tightened around his broad neck and shoulders as she pressed against his solid chest.

Margo lingered in the sensual embrace a few moments longer with no thought now for David's reaction. Perhaps a second or two too long, she realized as a cold trickle of common sense began seeping into her addled brain. She tried to pull out of the embrace but found herself locked firmly in the man's arms. When she struggled slightly, he finally surrendered his tantalizing possession of her lips. But she felt even more precarious as his arms relinquished their covetous hold to settle tenderly at her waist. Gasping for breath, she tried to get control of her still-reeling senses.

The stranger leaned back with the satisfied air of a job well done, and Margo stared into the darkest, sexiest eyes she'd ever seen and a face that took her breath away with its clean, hard lines and firm jaw. His gray-flecked dark hair was short and thick, and his right eyebrow was arched quizzically. No question about it: he looked amused.

"Thank you" was all she could manage.

"It says in the seminar schedule we're supposed to have live entertainment—is that you?" His resonant voice was fluid and deep. "Or are you the refreshments? If you are, I'd like to compliment the hotel."

One of the men at the nearby table, obviously a witness to the entire scene, laughed resoundingly. "I was starting to think the price of the seminar wasn't worth it!" He elbowed a balding man next to him in the ribs. "Better keep an eye out, Mike. The next one may be for you."

Margo's blush intensified. "Not quite," she muttered, keeping her voice low so that only he could hear her. "I was trying to...avoid someone."

She cast a wary look around and suddenly realized she hadn't been pursued. There was no sign of David, and that worried her. Her charade had been acted out for his benefit, in the hope it would provoke a confrontation that would spell out her feelings once and for all. It mystified her that he hadn't made a scene, but after such a display he couldn't possibly remain silent—not David Cort.

"Did it work?"

"Looks like it." Realizing she was still in his lap, she sprang to her feet as if she'd suddenly sat on a hot stove. "I'm terribly sorry about all this. Believe me, I don't usually run around throwing myself onto men's laps."

His mouth eased into a smile. A delicious twinkle glinted in his brown eyes. "Maybe you should do it more often. I, for one, can say it's quite a pleasurable experience."

Margo paused for a moment, unsure of her next move.

"What's wrong?" he asked.

Margo shrugged, perplexed. "Well, it's just that I hate to kiss and run, but—"

"Then don't."

The stranger wasn't smiling now. He was serious. With a blatantly appreciative look, his dark eyes took in her slim five-foot-four-inch frame—from her shoulder-length blond hair to her gray high-heeled shoes. It was a thorough look, more than surface deep, and the scrutiny made Margo uncomfortable.

"I really have to go," she said unsteadily. "The next lecture is about to start—"

"You could miss it," he said easily. "I know who's giving it. You'll do yourself a favor sitting it out; you'd only be bored. There's no reason to have your teeth put to sleep listening to somebody describing corporate taxes."

Margo didn't know how to respond. The idea of abandoning the lecture was enticing, but she'd paid dearly for it and the idea of throwing away her money grated on her. At the same time, it certainly wouldn't be a total loss to learn more about this attractive specimen of the male sex.

He stood, a six-foot-plus tower of strength and perfect muscle tone. He looked at home in a three-piece suit, Margo noted. Many of the other merchants were wearing idiotic video chain-store T-shirts blaring their logos and slogans for the world to see. But the idea of anything that crass or mundane on this man's pantherlike physique was an impossibility.

"Why don't we get out of here?" he suggested. "I don't particularly like the proverbial smoke-filled room."

Margo smiled and nodded, grateful for the suggestion. The heat was getting to her. But she feared it wasn't so much the smoke or the crowded room—it was him. She didn't know about the banquet hall, but *her* temperature had risen several degrees already. "Please, could we?"

The wide corridor, lined with openings to other rooms, all in use at the moment for seminar lectures, wasn't nearly as crowded. Margo looked in all directions before venturing too far. There was still no sign of David, and his absence was definitely suspicious. The David Cort she knew would have exploded at her crazy display of affection for a total stranger. A guardian angel must have smiled down on her for a change, she decided, relaxing in the knowledge that she'd escaped another of his marriage proposals. For a little while, at least, she would be spared his male chauvinism and dominating personality.

As the stranger steered her through the human obstacle course to an out-of-the-way alcove, she suddenly realized she hadn't even bothered to ask his name. Her gaze darted to the left side of his chest. No clue.

"You aren't wearing your name tag," she said accusingly.

"Neither are you," he countered. The smile returned to his lips.

"That's different," she said. "I have an excuse. I forgot to take it off before I soaked my blouse in my room's sink last night. Your turn."

"I don't lightly throw my name around. I don't need to."

Margo's eyes widened. "Does that mean you're trying to sound important, or you *are* important?"

"I *am* important—to the right people."

Margo laughed casually. "I have a feeling you want to remain anonymous. All right, go ahead. Maybe your wife is lurking around here somewhere—"

"No chance of that." He displayed his unadorned ring finger. Margo couldn't tell either from his tone or the look on his face whether he was joking. "Just call me Casey," he insisted.

"Just 'Casey'?" Margo asked with amusement.

"It'll do for now. It's what my friends call me."

Margo felt a familiar rush of color in her cheeks. "Well, I suppose after our little performance, I could honestly be called a friend." She produced her hand, and he shook it warmly, his powerful fingers surrounding her slender ones in a firm grip.

"Are you planning to tell me *your* name?" he asked, his eyes lazily retracing their earlier journey over her person. "Or is this just a one-sided deal?"

Again Margo felt uncomfortable under his scrutiny. I should have worn something else, she thought. This mousy gray business outfit would make even Carmen Miranda look dowdy. Why was it that three-piece business suits made women look like Miss Cardboard of 1988?

Margo found her voice and smiled. "I suppose I shouldn't be stingy. It's Margo. Margo Shepard—and people call me that whether they're friends or not."

Casey paused for what seemed an eternity. She thought she saw a glimmer of recognition in his dancing eyes, but then, her name wasn't exactly a secret. She'd made herself widely known at the seminar so far, handing out business cards right and left, hob-nobbing with many of the studio representatives and other merchants.

"You run your own store?" It was a casual, conversational question, but Margo thought she divined probing beneath his words.

"I *own*," she stressed, "Video Matinee up in Cielito Vista. We aren't an enormous monopoly, like some places I won't mention."

"Video Matinee..." Casey's features furrowed in thought. Up went that expressive right eyebrow of his. The name obviously meant something to him. He shook his head slowly in amusement, then laughed.

His reaction mystified her. She laughed uncertainly. "What's that supposed to mean?"

"Nothing," he managed to say. "Just a surprise, that's all."

"What? That I own my own store? Why should it be a shock?" Oh, God, she thought desperately, don't let Casey be another David—I've had enough women-shouldn't-be-in-business nonsense to last me a life-time.

"No shock," he assured her. "Just fate, I suppose."

"I assume you own your own store as well?"

"More than one, actually," he said vaguely. "I'm one of your 'unmentionables.'"

"Nobody's perfect," Margo allowed.

His attention shifted, and she realized he was looking past her to someone in the crowd. In the name of Cecil B. deMille, she pleaded silently, don't let it be David.

"Margo! I thought I'd never find you!" Jo's familiar voice was like music to her ears.

She was grateful to see her twenty-eight-year-old store manager approaching. Curly-haired, health-spa-toned Jo was a welcome sight, and Margo felt her features relax.

Jo gave Casey a smile and a nod of greeting, and her look was appreciative. "I'm glad to see that while I've been attending to business, you've found a little, yourself."

Margo tried to cover her blush with an unconvincing laugh. "Jo, I'd like you to meet Casey. Casey, this is Jo Bowden—Josephine, actually. She's my manager at Video Matinee."

"Pleased to meet you," he said warmly, extending his hand.

Jo took the hand offered her and pumped it in a businesslike manner. "Just Jo," she replied with a smile. "The last person who called me Josephine ended up in traction." She frowned slightly, looking from Margo to him. "Casey what?"

"Just Casey," Margo explained. "All his friends call him that." She fixed a reproving eye on him. "Besides, he doesn't have a name tag."

"What happened?" Jo asked, elbowing Margo. "He wash his blouse without taking the tag off, too?"

"Sin of omission," he said. "Forgot to put it on this morning." His eyes locked with Margo's, and their deep, probing look sent a thrill through her. "I'm glad I did, now."

Margo swallowed a lump in her throat. She wasn't sure whether it was from embarrassment, or...

Jo cleared her throat, rescuing Margo from having to respond. "You know, I hate to use my slingshot on any self-respecting friendship, Margo dear, but there's a lecture starting in—" she checked her digital wristwatch "—three minutes and twenty-seven seconds."

"I think lunch would be more rewarding," Casey said, his eyes not leaving Margo's.

"Lunch..." Margo said absently as his spell enveloped her. "Jo, I don't suppose you would—"

"Fill in," her manager finished with a sigh. "I understand. No problem. I'll meet you in our room after the lecture."

Margo tore her eyes away from Casey long enough to thank Jo. "You're sure you don't mind?"

Jo waved off the possibility. "Just remember me in your will."

As Jo threaded her way back into the crowd of merchants around the door of the banquet hall and disappeared from sight, Casey cleared his throat.

"Forgive me if I'm prying, but I couldn't help but notice: ever since fortune dropped you into my lap, you seem to be running away from something—or rather some*one*. Mind if I ask who?"

Margo swallowed. "No one, really," she said in a deliberately offhand manner. "I just have a persistent pest and I have the darnedest time finding a pesticide service."

"I think that means I won't find out."

"I think so, too." She had to change the subject. It was idiotic to stand here talking about David in the company of a man who could have walked out of a dream. "You mentioned lunch...."

"And I'm a man of my word," he said, slipping his arm smoothly beneath hers with a practiced grace.

Margo's spine buzzed with the same electricity that had jolted her when she'd first flopped into his lap and felt his powerful arms encircle her. This mystery man did something to her that she didn't understand, but as long as he was touching her she wasn't going to interfere with the magic. It was a wonderful, indefinable something that she'd never felt under the yoke of David's blatant possessiveness. She'd be a fool to stop it now.

The corridor to the elevators teemed with merchants rushing in last-minute sprints to attend lectures, but Margo could barely be bothered to notice them. The masculine pressure on her right arm and the slight, tantalizing brush of their thighs as he deftly led her toward the elevators was the only reality for her now.

Casey turned his movie-star face with its finely honed features to look at her, amusement playing across his lips and sparkling in his dark eyes.

"You look like you're in another world," he said. His voice was deep and dynamic even when he spoke softly. "A penny for your thoughts."

Margo swallowed. *I can't just blurt out that he's melted me like butter in a hot skillet,* she thought desperately. She attempted a halfhearted grin.

"I was just thinking," she said, feigning a reach into her memory, "that something like this happened to Norma Shearer in a movie once."

"Did it?" Only two words, but sensuality dripped from them.

Her flustered response came out hastily. "It may have been Joan Fontaine—I'm not sure."

The doors to the elevator slid open, delivering hotel guests to the ground floor, and Casey propelled her toward it.

"Maybe," he said, gently pulling her in to join the other passengers for the next trip to the top. "But I have a feeling this version won't be rated G."

As she understood his meaning, Margo's eyes widened and at that moment the polished brass elevator doors closed, as if to punctuate his words.

Chapter Two

The penthouse restaurant was elegant. Kentia palms, white latticework and baize green carpets spread before them. Even now, an hour before the normal lunchtime, the tan leather booths were full. In cozy, intimate nooks lining one wall, Margo spied several couples with their heads close together.

They were met in the foyer by a tall, slender maître d' whose stiffness and air of propriety suggested he wouldn't move a refined muscle even if a bomb were to explode in his elegant domain.

"Ah, a table for two—"

"Yes, Monte," Casey interjected hastily. He leaned over conspiratorially to the maître d', whispering something into his ear, and Monte responded with a diplomatic nod. "My usual table," Casey added.

"I understand, sir." He graciously indicated that Margo follow him. "This way, *madame*."

Margo hesitated a second, opening her mouth to question Casey about his whispered interchange with Monte. She closed it again when he put his finger to his lips.

"My secret for now," he said, eyes dancing. He motioned in the direction the headwaiter had taken. "Monte doesn't like to be kept waiting."

Margo did as she was told. As she followed the maître d' across the room, their path allowed her a good view of the lush interior of the restaurant. Casey was right behind her, his fingers lightly on her elbow, guiding her through the maze of tables and diners. The rich aromas of fine food drifted from every corner.

Monte ushered them to an out-of-the-way booth near the room's tall arched windows where carefully arranged potted palms afforded the spot a modicum of privacy. After producing a wine list for their perusal, Monte bowed and disappeared even before Margo was completely settled on the seat. Casey lowered himself into the booth beside her, and she felt their thighs touch.

The contact sent ripples of excitement through her. She watched him out of the corner of her eye as he opened the wine list and gave it a cursory scan. He knows what he's doing to me, she told herself. He knows and he's enjoying himself!

He'd remained in constant physical contact with her ever since they'd headed for the elevator: first her arm in his, then the gentle pressure of his hand around hers on the way to the top floor. As he had steered her through the maze of tables, she'd felt a moment of completeness. It seemed so right—his movements, his charming manners. A strange magnetism drew her to him, something that went beyond his charisma and cool demeanor.

Monte returned. After a thoroughly incomprehensible—to Margo—exchange of French with Casey, the maître d' collected the wine list, bowed again and was gone once more, leaving menus in front of them.

"I hope you don't mind my ordering something for you without asking," he said, his voice cool and relaxed. "They have a few wines I especially like here and I'd very much like you to try one."

"I'm impressed," Margo said. "A maître d' who knows you on sight, your own table, ordering wine in French—those people on TV aren't kidding. With an American Express card you *do* get treated right." He was smiling at her. "What is it?"

"You." Something in those profoundly dark eyes was laughing at her and seducing her at the same time. "I've never met anyone as completely and unabashedly responsive before. You're nothing like what I expected."

Margo's smile became a frown of puzzlement. "What you expected? You didn't even know me until twenty minutes ago. What could you possibly expect?"

"Not a witty, charming young woman—and certainly not a damsel in distress."

Margo blushed again. She'd have to stop being so affected by his wry comments or she'd spend the entire meal flashing like the red light on a fire engine.

"I said I was sorry about that—"

"I know," he said indulgently, nodding his head. "You were in flight from a persistent rodent...."

"Not a rodent, really," she allowed. "David's more like a lion—King of the Beasts."

"Okay, now I know his name is David. What else are you going to tell me about him?"

Margo had the maddening feeling she'd flicked the switch on the fire engine lights again. "That was sneaky. I said I didn't want to talk about it."

"*Its* name is David," he stressed, "and I think I have a perfect right to a complete explanation, seeing as he's responsible for the two of us having lunch together."

"You're nearly as persistent as he is," Margo said, exasperated.

He smiled. "I'm trying."

She opened her mouth to make a suitable rejoinder but was silenced by the arrival of the wine. Monte made a great show of displaying the label to Casey for approval, which he gave with a nod. The taste apparently met his standards, too, because Monte filled her tall glass three-quarters full with the honey-yellow Chardonnay and did the same for Casey before placing the bottle in a silver stand.

Margo was so entranced by the presentation of the wine that she started when Casey collected her menu before she'd even had a chance to open it. As he handed it back to Monte, he again spoke what seemed to her a veritable dictionary of French. Monte smiled widely and with another bow was gone.

"I assume that means you ordered lunch," Margo said wryly.

"A little something I think you'll enjoy."

Margo sipped the wine. Its amalgam of summer fruits was a sweet nectar. She let it pause on her tongue before swallowing it, noting its clean taste. Slightly dry with a delicate bouquet, she decided with satisfaction. Casey knew his wines.

Returning her glass to the table in front of her, she looked up into Casey's steady gaze. His expression was serious and unswerving.

"Come on, let's have the whole story."

Margo blinked. "The whole story...?"

"David," he coaxed. "You remember the story, don't you? It happened to you...."

"Oh, that story." Margo swallowed. She didn't really think he was interested. "I'm afraid it's a rather long one—"

"I like long stories," he assured her. "I sat through *Gone with the Wind* seven times, so I'm an old hand at this sort of thing."

Margo studied his face silently. She read nothing there. Did he really want to know? His tenacity on the subject counted for something, although David was one of her least favorite topics of conversation. She had been hurt—and the wounds of a first love hadn't completely healed yet.

Casey was waiting patiently, and she knew she had walked right into this one. Maybe if she told as little as possible she could satisfy his curiosity—without reopening the old injuries.

"David's my ex-fiancé," she said in a tone she hoped would convey most of her story without having to divulge too much. Her words sat in the air between them, no meaning attached, no interpretations offered.

After a moment, Casey cleared his throat, cocking his expressive eyebrow in mock understanding. "I see. I must say, that explains everything quite clearly. And it took you all of—" he checked his gold wristwatch "—about five seconds to tell. In fact, that has to be

the shortest long story I ever heard," he said, taking
a sip of his wine.

"That was the *Reader's Digest* condensed version." She looked down at the table and studied the
fine linen tablecloth. Her hands were clasped in front
of her, a portrait of tension. She just couldn't tell him
the details of her relationship with David.

From the minute they'd met at a Chamber of Com-
merce luncheon, she and David had been attracted to
each other. It was his handsome face and air of arrogant determination that had drawn her to him, and
being in the same business, they had hit it off immediately. There had been no way of knowing— Margo
suddenly noticed she was flexing her fingers, twisting
them nervously. Stress, she told herself: talking about
David always does this to me, even the thought—

"David just won't give up," she told Casey finally.
"We both went into the video business about three
years ago. His store is in Crystobal, near Cielito
Vista."

She looked up at him, hoping to see in his expression the evidence that he couldn't have cared less. No
luck: he appeared profoundly interested. But was that
interest for the story—or for her? She swallowed and
continued.

"We were together in this thing from the beginning—the same distributors, letting each other know
if anyone tried to rip off stores in the area. Eventually, we just sort of got together."

She cursed that day and her own stupidity. David's
attempts to control her had been subtle and innocent
enough to begin with. At first he'd merely decided
where they went for dinner or what movies they saw.
Then she gave in to his preferences in clothing and

makeup. She'd always hated browns, but buckled under for his sake; brown, David had said, was a man's color, and he liked to see it on his woman as sort of a trademark.

Margo shook her head to wipe the memory away. "I'm not boring you, am I?" she asked Casey, more casually than she felt. "If I am, I can talk about my appendix operation when I was twelve...."

"Just go on," he coaxed gently, his lips curving slightly. He leaned back in the booth, smoothly laying his arm along its back, near her neck.

"David sort of became my—what's the term?— 'main man,'" she said dubiously. "I only had eyes for him."

Her mind tried to blot out what had happened next in the relationship, but failed. Once the momentum had begun, denial of David's possessive nature had been nearly impossible. If she hadn't been so innocent and looking for a secure, fatherly image, she wouldn't have been so willing—or would she?

With almost mechanical precision, David had isolated her—physically and emotionally. He demanded that she stay home unless he escorted her, and any contact with the male sex—whether threatening to his romantic claim or not—was frowned upon. She'd never recovered from the embarrassment of David's jealous reaction when she'd gone out to lunch with a male representative from one of the studios. There had been no use telling David they were only discussing business. The studio rep never called the store again.

For reasons she couldn't completely understand now, she had given in to his manipulative demands. Somewhere along the line, Prince Charming had turned into Frankenstein's monster. Jo, her store manager, saw the stressful effects the relationship had on Margo, but advice from that corner had been ignored. Margo kept telling herself she was in love. Even when she cried.

"Everybody said we were a perfect couple," she told Casey with a shrug. "A nice girl like me hooking a hunk like David. And I have to admit—we *appeared* to be happy."

"Ah," Casey said, revelation evident in his voice. "I think we've reached a plot complication here. David wasn't such a hunk after all?"

She shook her head. "More like a crock."

Margo didn't know what had finally hit her over the head and given her a mind and will of her own. Maybe it was the garnet necklace he'd given her, expecting a long, drawn-out kiss as a reward for his generosity. Or was it when he'd made down payments on a house and furniture—before he'd even asked her to marry him? Things had moved too fast and furiously for her. The danger signals had all been there, and she'd finally recognized them. David's every action was designed with one goal in mind: to get her into his possession and into his bed. In his mind, love could be bought, and he'd found the price. Or thought he had.

That had to be what had brought her to her senses: she refused to be bought. If he thought laying gifts at her feet would make her long for the pleasure of his company, then he was sadly mistaken. The final blow came with his announcement that, after the wedding, he'd step in and run her store as well. She'd be staying at home. David wanted kids—a *lot* of kids.

Margo locked the odious memories away in a dark chamber of her mind. Never again, she promised herself. Not in a million years.

"David expected me to turn Video Matinee over to him after we were married," Margo heard herself say to Casey. "He was going to run 'our' two-store video empire while I sat at home producing little future video retailers. The feeling that I was being smothered by him was just too much."

Casey's right hand eased closer to hers. Her heart beat furiously as his index finger gently traced the contour of her thumb, sending a Morse code of warm sensations through her body. Her throat was suddenly very dry. How could the touch of one finger make her blood pulse like this? She noticed with surprise that she wasn't flexing her fingers anymore. Without even realizing he had done it, Casey had helped her survive the dangerous David Zone of her feelings.

"So, what did you do?" He wasn't looking at her; he was watching his finger's route across the back of her hand, as if visually taking in the sensuous feel of the contact. She suspected his intensely serious expression didn't have anything to do with her story.

"I did what any red-blooded American girl would do: I panicked. I walked out. Just like that."

"Just like that." He nodded affably. "And I'm sure David understood your reasons entirely...."

"If he had, would he still be asking me to marry him every fifteen minutes?" She laughed weakly. At least she could laugh about it now. Her flip comments and wry jokes amused Casey—just as they made others smile. But it still hurt; no brave front or defense mechanism could hide the inner damage. Thanks to David, the idea of a relationship with a man was infinitely threatening: there was no telling when Dr. Jekyll might turn into Mr. Hyde, and then the emotional roller coaster would begin again. Only she didn't intend to be around to witness the change. She held men at a distance now.

That is, she told herself, she had until now. Somehow Casey didn't provoke those defensive feelings. Maybe because he was a stranger, or perhaps it was a sign that her wounds had begun to heal. She went on, "David will make some poor girl a wonderful husband someday, I'm sure—but it won't be me. I'll never be that desperate."

"Then why does he chase you?" Casey's eyes weren't on their hands anymore. They were looking straight into hers, frankly curious, their dark depths asking more than his words.

Margo swallowed hard. Why was it so important to him? she wondered wildly. "We're supposed to be just good friends, now. Only I don't think he's quite gotten that into his head. He played football in college—maybe that explains it."

"Too many blows to the head? That would explain a lot of things."

"And so, that's all folks! You've heard the gruesomely tragic story of Margo Shepard's shattered love life. 'Film at eleven.'"

"What a poignant story." His eyes glittered with amusement. "But I can't bring myself to say I'm sorry it didn't work out."

"I still think I should have told you about my appendectomy when I was twelve," Margo said earnestly.

"So, then, I suppose that brings you to this morning. I was on the receiving end of another of David's ill-fated attempts at matrimony."

"It all makes sense. I had a couple of reasons for coming to the sales seminar, and David was one of them. I need to learn as much as possible about video merchandising just to show him how wrong he is about me."

"What was the other reason?"

"What? Oh, that. Basically, I'm trying to save my store."

Casey's eyebrow arched with greater interest. "Save it? Why, are you in financial trouble?"

Margo smiled circumspectly. "Company secrets, I'm afraid. No, I'm just trying to get some guy off my back—to get him to leave my poor store alone."

"*Another* man?" He couldn't hide a look of surprise behind his grin. "You have more mystery men in your life..."

Margo's blood pressure was rising. This subject always angered her, and now she felt the adrenaline flow freely. "He's no mystery. He's Kurtis Lawrence," she said furiously. "He owns the Hot Circuit Video chain and wants to buy my store. He has about a zillion outlets all over California and writes to me about buying my business, sight unseen. I've written and told him no a dozen times, but I keep getting proposals back in the mail...." Margo gritted her teeth in exasperation.

Casey's hand froze for a second, then it retreated slowly. He eased his arm from the back of the booth and rested his chin on his knuckles as a smile played at the corners of his mouth. "Come, now, a zillion seems a little exaggerated—"

"You know what I mean," she insisted. "He's got these ultra modern, crank-'em-out-as-fast-as-you-can video stores that cater to anyone with a fondness for rude employees and loud rock music."

"Why should he buy you out?" He ran one finger around the rim of his wineglass, then looked up at her inquiringly.

"I have my suspicions. He went into Santa Barbara a year ago and bought a little store, turning it into a carbon copy of his other stores. The main advantage was that he didn't have to start another store from ground zero—half the work had already been done for him: a good customer base, an extensive stock of movies. All he had to do was move in his Watta Wonder computer for rentals and install an eight-hundred-decibel stereo system."

Casey tilted his wineglass to his lips, sipping the contents sparingly. "Video's considered more than a small business these days. It's reached the corporate stage and needs to be run the right way."

"I bet you wouldn't stand for employees with purple hair and rings in their noses," Margo countered. "I kid you not! I was in one of his stores and actually saw a girl with a little gold ring on the side of her nostril! These big video stores have to do something or *they're* going to be in trouble."

"You seem to forget—I'm one of the 'unmentionables,' remember? I have fourteen stores." He looked at her evenly. It wasn't a challenging look, or playful. "And the bigger the stores, the more money they generate."

"Money isn't everything," Margo said simply. "I know no one goes into this business for their health, but we're also in it to serve the public. Come into my store sometime and I'll show you how to treat people. No wandering around like customers are forced to do in stores like Lawrence's. At Video Matinee we know many of our customers by name, and we use those names.''

His presence beside her was unsettling, not his sheer closeness, but the signals he was now putting out. They were so guarded compared to the openness he'd projected only minutes before. She'd done it again, she thought angrily. She'd gotten started on that tyrant, Lawrence, and ended up blowing it. It was always difficult to stop once she got started on Lawrence, Limited, and the corporate mentality.

"Where did you learn business?" Casey asked. "You have a most unique approach—at least for today's businesses."

"Right here," Margo said proudly, pointing to her head. "I get a lot more business sense out of *common* sense than I ever got in two years at the University of California at Santa Barbara."

"I can't believe you learned what you're telling me at UCSB. Is this your first business?"

"Yes, and there'll be more. Someday I'll have my own video empire. No one thought I would make it at first, but I literally built the business from nothing. When my father died four years ago, he left me enough to get the place started. I've always loved movies, and the video industry just sort of met me halfway—it was the logical thing to do. I found a vacant store and set up shop. Right from the start I brought in Jo—we were roommates in college. Her organizational skills are the best. I don't know what I would have done without her support, both emotionally and financially, and I'm glad she's seen our hard labor pay off.

"You've been successful, then . . ."

"I've made back my initial investment, yes." Margo nodded. "But with large chains moving into the area, I'm worried that Video Matinee may not withstand the competition they'll bring. I'm trying very hard to make it work. Everything I've made out of the store, I've put back in."

Casey's face was alive with curiosity. "Doesn't the word *profit* mean anything to you?"

"Profit will come. That's what happens when you build a business. Lawrence is in this principally for the fast buck: if it doesn't make money in thirty days, then out it goes. That's like the networks yanking a show off the air after two weeks because ratings didn't go through the ceiling."

"Interesting analogy," Casey mused.

"If he gets hold of my store, he'll want to spruce it up, give it a high-gloss look and sit back to see if it produces. If it doesn't, there goes all our work for nothing—another business chewed up and spit out by his video factory. But I refuse to let him do that to me. Dreams die hard—at least mine do."

Casey was silent for a moment. Too silent, Margo thought with a sinking feeling. She'd said too much, and—as usual—put too much fire and brimstone into it. Would she ever learn that men don't appreciate a verbal right hook?

Casey studied his wineglass again, as if its pale yellow depths could provide a reply. He refilled their glasses and looked up at her again. There wasn't a challenge in his eyes now—there was something else, something unfamiliar.

"Dreams *are* pretty important," he said huskily. "I guess I'd forgotten that a business really starts that way."

"Everybody has dreams," Margo said, enthusiasm for her favorite subject revitalizing her. Here was someone receptive to her ideas. "If I had the money, I'd have a video store like you wouldn't believe. No hard-sell stuff—and I admit there's some in my own store. You can't help it, what with displays screaming at you everywhere. I'd give the place a homier look, make it a place where you can get an evening's entertainment and see a few old friends at the same time."

As she spoke, she became more animated. She couldn't contain her excitement for her dream, and he was so sympathetic. "Remember the corner malt shop when you were a kid? That's what I'm aiming for. A section for the children, out of the way and all their own—kids like that."

Casey nodded thoughtfully, his deep gaze proving his interest. "I like the idea."

"Do you realize how boring plaster is?" she asked suddenly.

"Now that I think of it—" he smiled "—I'd have to admit it isn't high on my list of exciting things. Why?"

"I want the place to feel like the lobby of an old movie palace—like the Chinese Theater or something. With a marquee over the door," she emphasized, indicating the effect with her hands. "The store's name in lights—not the stupid signs the city sign committee recommends. God, there's so much more...." Her gesture hinted at the great untold vistas of her ideas.

His hands found hers, trapping them gently. "Okay, Cecil B. deMille," he said, laughing. "I can see the epic proportions."

His eyes met hers warmly, and she felt a silent bond between them. Her sense of kinship with this mystery man was growing as she felt his empathy for her Video Matinee dreams, and it was definitely more than just a meeting of minds over video stores. His touch kindled a fire in her veins and a knot in her stomach—maybe David hadn't been able to destroy her emotions entirely.

Margo blushed again, realizing she had monopolized the conversation. "You probably had some sort of picture of the future, too, with birds twittering on the edges of the frame and stuff like that. Except, when you opened your first store, you had no idea it would become—what? Fourteen stores? What's the name of your chain?"

Casey's eyes faltered for only a second, then looked past her, his face brightening. "I think lunch is here."

Margo forgot her question as a stiff and proper young waiter arrived with their lunch on a huge tray. He transferred steaming plates of fettuccine to the table with a flourish, and after receiving instructions from Casey, again in French, he disappeared among the tables and potted palms.

"If you keep speaking French," Margo chided, "I'm going to feel like I'm having lunch at the United Nations."

"Just another bottle of wine," Casey assured her. He checked their own bottle in its tableside ice bucket. "Apparently I'm not the only one who likes it."

"It's very good. I don't usually drink much, but I can appreciate a few glasses of an excellent wine on occasion."

"And I know just the occasion," he declared, filling her glass, then his own, with the remainder of the bottle and bringing his glass up in a toast. His sparkling eyes met hers over the rim. "Seven o'clock this evening? Dinner?"

Margo was surprised by the invitation. This little fantasy might actually last beyond the bill at the end of the meal. Could it become even more interesting? Would dinner be a feast for the senses, bringing her emotions to the surface for a taste of excitement and romance? She pictured Casey close to her in the booth, a warm, intimate dinner by candlelight—maybe even an embrace? Her expression must have gone blank for Casey was waving his long-fingered hand before her eyes.

"Anyone home?" he asked.

Margo blinked, giving him her full attention. She smiled widely, bringing her wineglass up to meet his. "Thank you very much, Casey," she smiled. "I'd love to."

Margo felt reassured. A teasing glint was in his eyes again. He closed a warm hand over hers, and her arm seemed to melt from the fingers upward. A blazing sensation that felt almost like panic raced through her body. This was a dangerous moment, considering her past romantic injuries. She'd reentered the sexual arena whether she'd intended to or not.

But no one had ever made her feel this way before, she realized. She liked him very much, cynical demeanor and all. His combination of warm understanding, dry wit and masculine charisma were irresistible. As she ate, Margo took a good, long look at him.

His gray-flecked dark hair was immaculate and thick. The clean line of his strong, angular jaw gave a determined cast to his face. His dark eyes, always full of amusement, sought hers repeatedly, and more than once she averted her gaze to the food on her plate, not wanting to be caught looking at him. What thoughts could he read in her hazel eyes? she wondered, and were her feelings so obviously displayed?

She looked away from his probing gaze again, glancing down the aisle, and at once her thoughts froze. Halfway to her mouth, her fork became immobile. A sudden dryness constricted her throat, making it impossible for her to issue the warning that sprang to her lips. A hollow opened in the pit of her stomach, and she felt the familiar pangs of panic. The only thing to do was to sink slowly and gracefully under the table.

Casey was aware of her sudden change in mood.

"Margo, is anything wrong?"

She didn't have time to warn Casey of the approach of all six feet two inches of dark-haired, infuriatingly precise, always conservatively dressed David Cort. He wasn't aware of her yet, but it was just a matter of seconds before he passed the table. Jo was trailing in his imposing wake.

David spotted Margo from ten yards away, and the expression on his face was terrible to behold. He stalked to the table in a fury, with Jo tagging along, a comic look of distress on her face.

"There you are!" He crammed into those three little words all the frustration of the hour or so he'd searched for her in vain.

He was really furious, Margo realized. One lock of his carefully combed dark hair had fallen on his forehead and—horror of horrors—his vest was unbuttoned. She couldn't recall ever seeing David in any situation that required the drastic step of unbuttoning his vest.

Jo gave Margo a pitiful look. "Margo, when I suggested we come up here, I had no idea—"

David paid no attention to Casey. All his rage and inappropriate jealousy were directed at Margo. "A fine thing: I run all over the damned hotel to find you and all the time you're having lunch with another man. And don't think I didn't see you downstairs clutched in the passionate embrace of some two-bit video hustler."

Margo was speechless. David was finally making a scene. But this was all wrong, she realized in agony. Not now—not here, with Casey. Controlling her natural impulse, she refrained from giving him a swift high heel to the shins to shut him up. There was no point in reacting on his level, she told herself.

"The only reason I didn't do or say anything at the time," he said blackly, "was because I had to introduce the president of the Videocassette Dealers Association. A man can take only so much betrayal—" He stopped abruptly, aware of her lunch partner for the first time. "Oh, my God, I don't believe this!"

Margo finally found her voice. David had to be brought under control. "David, please, this isn't what you think—"

"It isn't, is it? Talk about going behind a guy's back—this beats them all!"

Margo began to stand up, then thought better of it. No need to let everyone in the restaurant see another member of this impromptu cast of characters.

"David, I refuse to explain my actions to you when—"

"I don't need any explanations," he growled. His gaze shifted to Casey. "I've heard of double crosses before, but never a *double* double cross!"

"No one's double-crossing anyone," Jo interjected diplomatically. She tried to move David away, but the strength she'd gained from eighteen months at a local gym and her usual ten-mile daily jog weren't enough to budge David Cort once he'd put down roots. The irresistible force had met an immovable object. "David, they're just having lunch together."

"That's all," Margo pleaded softly. If she hadn't been so angry, she would have cried—this was so like David.

She looked to see the effect of his performance on Casey and detected a definite air of contempt.

"So, *this* is your David," Casey said. He nodded coolly at the other man. "Small world, isn't it?"

"What?" Margo did a double take. Casey spoke as if he knew David. She turned a wild, questioning look on her lunch companion. "Just what's going on? Do you know David?"

Casey's teasing smile became enigmatic. "We've met, all right."

"That's right," David fumed. The animosity she read in his blue eyes was frightening. "It wasn't enough that I ordered you and your propositions out of my store less than two weeks ago—now you're wining and dining my girl into the same sort of agreement!"

Margo finally stood up, unable to endure any more. "Wait just a minute!" she said to David. "First of all—I am *nobody's* 'girl.' If I choose to go to lunch with Arnold Schwarzenegger or Paul Newman, it's none of your business." She whirled on Casey. "Second—who are you and what is all this about?"

Casey had been casual so far and even now, on the threshold of some sort of revelation, he remained unflappable. He nonchalantly reached into the inside breast pocket of his gray pinstriped jacket and withdrew a business card, presenting it to her with a modest bow of the head.

"My card, Miss Shepard."

The corporate logo of Lawrence, Limited, glared from the card. Bold script proclaimed, "Kurtis Charles Lawrence, President."

Not Casey, but K.C. Kurtis Charles—Lawrence. She froze. Shock prevented her from saying anything. Kurtis Lawrence took another sip of wine, looking self-assured and confident. Suddenly she wanted to scream.

The men's verbal battle, punctuated by comments from Jo, raged around her, but she refused to listen. Then the full impact of the situation hit her, and she felt sick. The whole thing had been a charade from the beginning—not on her part, she realized, but on his. The things she'd told him—confidential things about herself and about the store . . . she'd all but given him the keys to Video Matinee and let him walk off with it! *And* he'd kissed her.

Oh, God—how he'd kissed her. The closeness of their bodies in the elevator, the brush of his thigh against hers, his tender hand-holding . . . The tears finally welled in her eyes as anger and all her old feelings about men and relationships flooded back. Twice stupid, she screamed at herself. She had been right to begin with: romance was dangerous. Too dangerous for her. "Casey"—or Kurt—was just like David, after all. He'd known all along what he was doing to her, what he was hoping to gain. She was the supreme sucker.

Margo's fingers started to flex again, and this time David had nothing to do with it. She wanted to slap smug Kurtis Charles Lawrence, give him a round-house with her purse—there was a good reason she kept a roll of quarters in her bag, and it wasn't to feed washers at the Laundromat back home! No, no, that wouldn't be enough, she decided.

It was a lightning move, a reflex action inspired by frustration and vengeance for her sex. No one had time to stop her. She didn't give Kurt Lawrence the chance to dodge her unfinished plate of fettuccine Al-fredo. With a resounding smack and a splatter range of several feet, noodles and sauce drenched his jacket and vest, then slid onto his lap, splaying in a glorious abstract mess across the legs of his carefully tailored trousers. Stray missiles of cheese splattered the tan leather booth and the tabletop, creating a work of modern art worthy of the Metropolitan Museum.

Margo didn't wait for the reaction—not from Jo, not from David or the other patrons and especially not from Kurtis Lawrence. Casey, indeed! Ignoring Jo's look of open-mouthed horror, Margo grabbed her store manager by the arm, dragging her unceremon-iously away, as David trailed behind, stunned out of his rage.

Margo stepped into the waiting elevator and vi-ciously punched the button for the ground floor. She saw Monte heading toward Kurt Lawrence's table, a pile of towels in his arms, but he didn't even raise an eyebrow.

Chapter Three

Margo stepped into the foyer of the penthouse restaurant that evening and froze when she saw the maître d' at his podium. She felt no remorse for Kurt Lawrence's humiliation, but she was sure Monte's day had been a rough one.

Still he wouldn't have to worry about any instant replays: she was dining alone to avoid any more of David's tirades, and Kurt Lawrence would undoubtedly see the wisdom of breaking their dinner date after his lapful of fettuccine. She'd urged Jo to have a night on the town, and her manager had gladly headed for the Dorothy Chandler Pavilion to take in the latest musical. Being alone this evening was important to Margo; the day's events needed to be sorted out, and the company of others would just complicate things.

Have courage, she urged herself, making sure the sleek lines of her black evening gown were correct. Its neckline was cut daringly low, displaying the fullness of her breasts, and it was virtually backless, exposing the tanned slope of her back. She felt sophisticated in the dress, and a single strand of pearls was the only ornamentation she needed. The gown made her feel sexy and confident and feminine—just the way she wanted to feel tonight, after her display at lunch.

Monte's placid, deferential air never wavered. He raised his head, giving her a wide, welcoming smile and a reverent nod of recognition.

"Ah, you return to the scene of the crime," he said smoothly. "The same table?" he asked without blinking an eye.

"Good evening, Monte," she managed, sure the blush rising in her face was in glorious contrast to her black gown. "I made a reservation for one—for seven o'clock. Shepard," she added helpfully, realizing he hadn't learned her name on her first, ill-fated visit.

"Yes," he confirmed, after scanning his reservation list. "I have it here. If Miss Shepard will follow me..."

Margo fell into step behind Monte as she had done only a few short hours ago, and a disconcerting attack of déjà vu came over her. Only something was missing: the lack of Kurt Lawrence's vital presence beside her was terribly obvious. There was no manly grasp guiding her with practiced ease among the tables, and the masculine sensuality that had followed her every step was gone.

Monte seated her in a small alcove, open to the main aisle of the restaurant. She told herself to be realistic. This isn't lunch—lunch is a million miles away now.

Monte produced the wine list with his usual aplomb, but Margo waved it aside, asking for a glass of the wine Kurt had ordered at lunch. With a bow, Monte was gone.

It wasn't cheating, she told herself firmly. Her selection of wine had nothing to do with lunch or with Kurt Lawrence. She liked the wine, as she'd told him honestly, and felt no awkward compunction about drinking it without his company.

I must make a fine picture here, alone—looking like a widow dressed in black, hiding in an alcove, she thought ruefully. If she added a wide-brimmed hat and a long cigarette holder, she would resemble a poisonous mystery woman from a forties' Bogart movie. All you gotta do is whistle, she replayed from memory.

"Ditch that," she muttered to herself, sipping at her glass of water. "I can't whistle."

Monte returned with her wine and stood ready to help her make her selection from the menu but she only skimmed the many entrées available.

"Can you suggest anything, Monte?"

"Everything is superb, Miss Shepard," he said smoothly. "Since you are dining alone this evening," he added, "perhaps you would like to try the fettuccine Alfredo again?"

Margo closed the menu, a beaconlike flush coloring her cheeks again. "Anything will be fine, Monte— except that. I'll trust your judgment."

With a conciliatory bow, Monte was gone again.

Margo took stock of her surroundings. The table was well placed, giving her a good view of the dining room and its occupants. Potted palms screened tables on either side of her, as did the high-backed booths that encircled the tables on her side of the room. Kurt's table was out of sight, but not out of mind. Is he sitting there now? she wondered. Is he eating alone, fully aware that a lapful of fettuccine had spelled the end of his proposed date? Could he take that subtle a hint?

Margo had an urge to stand up and peer over the many heads and palm fronds to see him, but resisted it. She told herself she didn't want to know, then, with a sigh she admitted that she *did*. Was he sitting there waiting for a dinner partner who would never show up? Or was he acting as if he didn't have a care in the world, his charade at lunch just an amusing deception?

To heck with restraint, she told herself grimly. Getting to her feet as unobtrusively as possible, she jockeyed for a view of Kurt's table. A young couple was seated there, their heads close together and smiles on their faces. So, one evening's preempted conquest gave way to another, she thought. No—wrong table. She shifted her gaze to the next booth. Strategically placed palms marked the spot. It was empty.

Deep down she'd known he wouldn't be there, but just the same it was a strange disappointment to find the booth vacant. With a resigned sigh, she settled back into her seat. At least they'd been able to clean up the mess.

She reached for her glass and tilted it to her lips, taking a sip of the delicious wine. Suddenly she choked on it, lowering the glass quickly to the tabletop in amazement as she saw David homing in on her booth.

"Margo! I've looked everywhere for you."

She closed her eyes in frustrated resignation, bending her head into her hands. She felt a surge of panic— a common reaction when confronted with David. Why me? she thought miserably. Why the ten plagues of David?

She raised her head, smiling weakly as he came up to the table. He was dressed for a funeral, as usual, she noted—his dark blue pinstripe made him look the epitome of the Republican party member. He looked dashing and successful—and dangerous.

He wore a look of concern. "You aren't eating alone?"

"That was the idea," Margo muttered, averting her eyes and studying her wineglass. What would she do if he sat down? Please, God...

"We'll have to remedy that," he said confidently, slipping into the booth beside her. The seat wasn't large to begin with, and David's wide shoulders and powerhouse frame took up more than their share of space. Margo slid out of range. "Cozy, isn't it?" David winked pleasantly.

Margo was silent. Angry words rose in her throat, but she couldn't bring herself to fling them at him. I don't want you here, she wanted to scream. Can't you leave me alone? She told herself not to cry, for she knew he would love that. Then he could be tender and caring, and then afterward he would want—what? There was always a string attached somewhere.

"I won't have my girl eating in a posh restaurant all by herself. It isn't right." He turned in his seat, searching for a waiter.

She could not endure dinner with David. He had that paternal, protective look in his eyes that meant she had been right: he was on the marriage bandwagon again, and his ace in the hole would be the fiasco earlier in the day. Margo firmly decided not to listen.

"Pardon me," she said pointedly, distracting him from his search for the hired help, "but just how did you know I was up here?"

"That was easy, honey." David's crooked smile appeared above a chin with a deep cleft. "I know women like the back of my hand. Your kind sticks close to home, whether you're traveling or not. You wouldn't wander around L.A. to find someplace to eat. You'd eat right here." He leaned back in satisfaction, obviously pleased at his less than spectacular display of detection.

"Besides," he nudged her elbow gently with his beefy forearm, "I came up here for dinner anyway and saw you peeking over those plants. I could tell you were looking for me."

Margo took a hearty gulp of wine. Steady, old girl. Of all the arrogant, self-centered... Her thoughts petered out.

"Where *is* that waiter?" David asked, turning in his seat again to peer down the aisle. He turned back to her. "You know, it shows a lot of guts for you to come back up here for dinner after lunch today."

"David, really, I..."

"No, it does," he emphasized. "That creep Lawrence deserved every noodle you dumped on him. I'd have laid him out on the carpet, but you beat me to it. That's one I owe him. You don't need to worry your little head about him—not with me around."

She gritted her teeth. "I'm *not* worried, David—"

"Of course," he continued with a frown as if she hadn't said anything, "that still doesn't excuse your getting tangled up with him. I'm surprised at you—after all we've meant to each other." He held up one ruddy hand to silence her reply and hung his head sadly. "Don't say it; it won't help. I know there's no excuse in the world for that amorous display with him downstairs this morning, but I forgive you, just the same," he said magnanimously. "I can't hold it against you...not the woman I love—"

She was going to cry. Despite her best efforts, she couldn't hold back the tears anymore. She turned her head away, as if taking in the room's decor. Why did she feel so helpless around him? Past hurts kept her from thinking clearly whenever David showed up, and she never seemed to have the courage just to tell him to go to hell.

Blinking back a tear, she decided to do it. If there was one good thing about this whole day it would be the satisfaction she'd get from telling David Cort to go jump in the lake. She had to get rid of him. She couldn't endure any more conversation about marriage or the encounter with Kurt Lawrence. Most of all, she couldn't endure him.

"David..." Margo began, turning to face him. She paused, hoping her earnest expression would make an impression on his thick skull. "I intend to eat alone."

A vague looked passed over David's chiseled features. His eyes went down in a familiar hurt-little-boy look that she recognized as one of his ploys. He'd tried to get more than dinner out of her with that look before. "Jeez, Margo—I just want a nice, romantic evening with you, you know. I mean, you're a woman and I'm a man, after all. And I've got something to ask you—"

"The answer is no," Margo said firmly for the thousandth time. "I want a little time alone. It's been a long day and I'm tired. Can't you let a starving woman eat in peace?"

"You wouldn't *be* starving if you'd gone to lunch with *me*," he said suddenly. "You should know by now that you're vulnerable—"

"David, stop," she said with finality. "If you want to stay here, that's fine with me." She slipped out of the booth and got to her feet. "I'll leave you alone and then I can have a nice quiet evening. You forget, we all have to get up early for the last day of lectures."

"No, no," David said with deep resignation, rising and waving her back into the booth. "Stay here. I'll let you eat by yourself. But I want to talk to you when we get back home." His heavy brows were furrowed in concern. "After today, I think you'll agree—you need me around to keep you out of trouble."

"I don't need you to keep me out of anything," Margo protested. "I'm perfectly capable of taking care of myself, thank you. And don't give me that look, either!" she warned. She'd do it. She'd tell him to go to hell. "Look, David, go to—go have a nice time this evening. Jo's seeing a play at the Dorothy Chandler Pavilion. You still have time to catch a cab, and she'd enjoy the company."

Forgive me, Jo, Margo thought wildly. All I know is I have to get rid of him before I go crackers.

"I'll go," David assured her. He clamped her hands in an iron grip, giving her his version of a tender look. "I *do* want to talk with you."

After he released her hands and wound his way out of sight among the potted palms and restaurant patrons, Margo expelled a long sigh of relief. She mentally kicked herself, draining her glass of wine to steady her jangled nerves. She'd chickened out at the last minute—on the last word. Spying Monte passing a few tables away, she signaled to him. He came to her table immediately.

"I have a feeling I'll need the bottle, Monte." Monte bowed and was gone again.

"Why not share mine?"

She couldn't mistake *that* voice. A chill, electric shock ran up Margo's spine, sending tingles to the farthest reaches of her body. She felt paralyzed. Surely she was dreaming—or at least indulging in a little wishful thinking.

Twisting sharply in her seat, she strained her neck to discover the truth and found herself staring into the laughing eyes of Kurt Lawrence. He was leaning over the tan leather back of the booth, propping himself on his elbows with an infuriating casualness.

Margo found her voice, but it came out choked and erratic. "You!"

His right eyebrow lifted and he gave her a dazzling smile. "Mind if I join you?"

Before she could make any protest, his head disappeared from over the back of the booth and suddenly he was standing, wineglass in hand, in the aisle in front of her.

"I said dinner at seven." Mischief played in his dark eyes. "You're late."

Margo swallowed her unspoken words—along with a hard knot in her throat. His athletic, commanding body was clad in finely tailored black evening clothes, as crisp and elegant as if he were about to meet royalty, not merely spend the evening in a restaurant. The lights from the chandeliers made the scattering of gray in his hair sparkle like reflections off rippling water.

"I'm not late," Margo managed defensively. "I've been here all along."

He slid deftly into the booth beside her, as sleekly as a panther. He even looked like one in his evening clothes.

"That's right," he said. "I forgot—everything is my fault today." He fixed her with that look again. "Only I have a bone to pick with you."

"Me?" Margo started as if she'd been stuck with a pin. "*You* were the snake in the grass!"

"I'm referring to the bruises you inflicted." His voice was cool and smooth as he leaned forward on his elbows, crossing his arms. His deep, dark gaze was steady.

"Bruises! I smacked you with a plate of noodles! If you want bruises, I can give them to you without any culinary intervention."

"I'm talking about bruises to my ego." The teasing twinkle returned to his eyes.

Margo reached for her wineglass and laughed sarcastically. "Well, I'm sure you didn't feel much. There's quite a bit of it to bruise. As a matter of fact," she said, sipping her wine and returning the glass to the table, "it could stand with a little reductive surgery."

Monte returned, bringing the bottle of wine, and placed it in an ice bucket stand beside the table. In a low voice, Kurt instructed the maître d' to have his dinner sent to her table—they would be dining together. For a second, Margo thought she detected a look of surprise on Monte's imperturbable countenance. Then, he was gone.

Kurt was silent a few moments, then said solemnly, "I *am* sorry about lunch today. I had no intention of leading you on like that. It's not my style to play games with a woman, especially one as attractive as you.''

Margo looked desperately into the depths of her glass, grateful she could hold on to it so he wouldn't see her hands shaking. Her pulse was pounding heavily, and her anger was hard to hold onto. She felt an uncomfortably hot flush on her skin, knowing his penetrating eyes were boring straight through her mask of coldness. His words were sweet, sensual and spoken with an honesty that unnerved her. What was happening to her? She should be furious with him— but the dictates of her body beat the anger down.

She'd been silent too long. He leaned over, trying to look into her eyes. ''Anybody home, or is this space for rent?''

Margo smiled halfheartedly, giving a weak laugh. ''Pretty rotten thing to do, you know. Flatter the queen of the witty rejoinders—that's not fighting fair.''

''Who says we have to fight?'' He tenderly clasped her left hand, bringing it to his lips and giving it a gentle kiss. ''A humble apology to my lady fair.''

The warm touch of his lips on the back of her hand struck the death knell of her resistance and sent a searing jolt of feeling through her. Suddenly she felt as if her skin were on fire. She paid no attention to the warning bells in her head: her senses were all focused on him, and it could have been lunch, before his unmasking, all over again. She tried to be serious, but pinpricks of expectation made that difficult.

''Come on, now, Mr. Lawrence—''

''Casey, if you don't mind,'' he interjected.

Margo sighed in irritation. ''Are you going to start that again?''

"I mean it. Casey's my nickname."

"All your friends call you that," Margo added skeptically.

"And I still consider you a friend," he said, the lights from the small candle on the table flickering in his rich, dark eyes.

"I think I'll stick with Kurt. Neither one of us has to play dumb."

"I wouldn't work that way with you," he said.

"But our stores . . ." Margo tried.

"I think we can leave the stores out of this to-night." His eyes were deep and enticing. "We're two people sitting in this booth—not two stores."

Margo was at a loss for words. Her intention of fighting a battle to the death with him fizzled with his refusal to discuss the subject. Her heart pounded at his closeness in the small booth, and she savored the heady, musky aroma of his cologne. Inbred survival instincts warned her repeatedly that this man could turn her toiled-for dream into a nightmare, but something stilled the call to alarm.

The arrival of dinner rescued her from having to reply. A heavyset waiter placed steaming plates of veal scaloppini and chicken *cordon bleu* before them. Monte hovered attentively in the background to make sure all went as planned. When the waiter departed, he came forward.

"I've given Miss Shepard the chicken *cordon bleu*, " he announced formally. "I hope she enjoys it." He turned to Casey, sensing that command would now come from him. "Will there be anything else, Mr. Lawrence?"

"You might make sure you have a good supply of this wine," he advised, checking the bottle in the tableside holder. "My favorite's pretty popular this evening." He slid a sly glance at Margo.

Margo self-consciously lowered the goblet from her lips, wondering if she hadn't had too much to drink already. She felt warm and light-headed. It had to be the wine, she reasoned. But she knew that was a lie. Despite her best efforts to remain businesslike and unmovable, Kurt was affecting her the same way he had affected her at lunch. His nearness, the heady aroma of his cologne and his undeniable charisma were intoxicating.

Satisfied that Kurt and Monte were suitably engaged in a wine discussion, Margo let her eyes slide carefully to her left thigh. Kurt was only a fraction of an inch away. His warmth penetrated through the thin material of her black evening sheath, and she suddenly felt exposed. The sophisticated dress left little to the imagination. Her racing pulse fed off his closeness, and his powerful hands with those strong, capable fingers were just a handclasp away. Was she clutching the stem of her wine glass almost desperately, or was it her imagination?

"Monte will keep us well supplied," she heard Kurt say. "And you said you didn't drink much wine..."

His voice pulled her back to reality. Monte had left, and Kurt was sitting much too close beside her. His beautiful dark eyes were regarding her with a mixture of amusement and determination. Forcing her attention away from him, she tried to concentrate on the food.

As Margo took her first bite, she warned herself to stay on her toes this evening. Without question, Kurt had a disturbing effect on her, and she might not be as cautious as she should be. She would have to keep the conversation directed away from herself.

She swallowed. "You know, we've done an awful lot of talking about me," she pointed out. "Why don't we probe your life for a change? Turnabout is fair play."

Kurt paused, a forkful of veal halfway to his mouth. A mischievous smile crossed his face. "I thought you knew all about me: the big video baron with more stores and money than he knows what to do with, running around California, gobbling up poor innocent businesses right and left . . ."

"I'm talking about the sordid details," Margo said.

"All right," Kurt allowed with a laugh. "I'll admit it—I started small with a one-store operation in the San Fernando Valley. God, it must have been almost five years ago, now. That's where it all began."

"That's only the first store. One down, plenty to go . . ."

"Well, one thing just followed another. The first store became so busy and successful, that I had to open another and then another and . . ."

"And another and another . . ." Margo echoed.

Kurt shrugged complacently. "I couldn't help it: it just sort of happened. Kind of like all the 'begatting' in the Bible. We just kept growing—and we'll continue to grow," he added firmly.

"It sounds like a disease," Margo said ruefully.

"Now, come on, Margo," he said seriously. "You said yourself this afternoon that you wanted a video empire of your own."

"Well, I'm seriously reconsidering it. After all, it would just be one more place for you to try to buy out from under me."

"All right, little feline," he said, settling his right hand over her left one, "pull in your claws. No fighting at dinner—that's an order."

Suddenly the food in her mouth had no taste as all of her senses focused on the strong, masculine pressure of his hand on hers. The blood pounded in her veins and she knew she was falling under his spell again, but she couldn't bring herself to escape its powerful hold. She was confused, not sure whether she wanted to escape or not. Through a thickening mental haze, she saw his face turned to her inquisitively. Did it also hold concern?

"Are you all right?" he asked.

She brought her napkin out of her lap, lightly fanning herself with it. "Is it warm in here, or is it just me?"

A subtly familiar smile flowed across his face. "I think you could honestly say that the temperature *is* rising, yes."

Dear Lord, Margo thought swallowing a lump in her throat.

"Go on—please don't let me stop you," she babbled. "By all means... You were doing so well...." Please, she thought desperately, keep talking. She returned her napkin to her lap and reached for her glass of ice water.

His amusement was evident from the deepened laugh lines at the corners of his eyes. She hadn't noticed them before, she thought, bemused.

"I grew up in, shall we say, privileged circumstances. Mom and Dad were well-off. Dad was in commercial construction—hotels, that sort of thing. I left home at seventeen. I wanted to make it on my own without the help my father tried to shove down my throat.''

"Seventeen is awfully young, isn't it?"

Her words faltered. His index finger traced a further exploration on the smooth skin of her forearm. Concentration on his story was impossible. All she was aware of was the exquisite burst of sensation the mere touch of a finger could bring—much more of this would turn her into a mass of quivering jelly.

"When it's necessary, it's necessary," he said philosophically. "I went to work for an uncle in Santa Barbara, helping him run a small store. That's where I got interested in retail. I saved enough money to go to community college and get a degree in business. No MBA, but it was a start.''

He moved even closer to her, though Margo thought it impossible. His thigh was firmly pressed against hers, forcing them to share space, warmth and sensation.

"And I'll bet you're good at starting things...." Margo commented. Overwhelming emotions rocketed through her with a fierce and frightening intensity.

Kurt acknowledged this comment with another tilt of his eyebrow and continued. "I opened the first store on a wager from my Uncle John: he'd bet if I went into the video business, I'd lose my shirt within the year. I damned near did," he smiled. "Video was a new business and there was no background, no test stores to go against. I was flying blind—but I did it. I won the bet. The profits paid for the second store.''

"And thus the 'Birth of a Nation'—or, at least, an empire.'' Margo said wryly. Setting her fork in her plate, she sat back, consciously pulling her hand out of his tender grasp. "I guess I'm not as hungry as I thought," she explained lamely.

"That's too bad," he said, putting down his fork and leaning back as well. "Dinner is delicious."

"Oh, I know it is, it's just . . ." Her voice trailed off helplessly. Just what?

"And may I say you look particularly beautiful tonight?"

Margo swallowed. "Thank you. You're rather—beautiful, yourself."

His hand found hers again. Like metal to a magnet, her eyes were drawn to his. "You know, I like you, Margo. You're a levelheaded woman. You're smart, attractive, and you have a sense for pleasing people. Any one of the three would impress me, but all of them together make you downright irresistible."

Margo averted her eyes to his strong fingers intertwined with hers, not knowing whether to feel pleased or patronized. He didn't sound as if he were patronizing her. If she just wasn't so confused! She didn't know him—not really. They'd only met this morning . . . and flying fettuccine probably wasn't conducive to lasting friendships. But she felt strangely drawn to him. She knew a lot of caution was indicated where Kurt Lawrence was concerned, but there was also much to admire.

Margo found her voice. "I have a feeling we're a lot alike." Her gaze came up. "Whatever I may have thought of you, you're certainly charming."

Kurt presented her with a smile of genuine pleasure.

He was even closer now, and the searing warmth in her veins begged to be diffused. The closer she got to Kurt, the nearer she came to an emotional breaking point. She tried to remind herself that that point shouldn't be reached. Because of their professional roles, it wouldn't be right, no matter how she felt about him. She had to escape.

From a far corner of the restaurant she detected music, something with a lilting, Big Band dance rhythm. "Either someone's playing music," she said, "or I'm living in a movie."

"That's the Deco Room," Kurt replied. "They have a dance floor."

"I absolutely love Big Band music," Margo confessed, leaning back. Maybe, just maybe, she could bring her emotions under control with a change of subject. "I was born in the wrong era."

Kurt's chiseled features softened in amusement. "Far be it from me to deny a misplaced spirit what she holds dear to her heart. May I indulge you by asking for this dance?"

Margo swallowed nervously. His offer was the last thing she'd expected, but after her praise for the music, it would be awkward to refuse. He slid out of the booth and straightened his dinner jacket then reached down for her hand. She gave it gingerly as he helped her to her feet. They weren't two yards from the table before Monte reappeared, concerned.

"Everything is all right, Mr. Lawrence?"

"Of course, Monte," Kurt assured him. "We're headed for the Deco Room."

The maître d' nodded. "Very good, sir." He turned to check the table, then as an afterthought, he added, "Will you be requiring a towel this evening?"

"Just put this on my bill," Kurt said firmly.

"Yes, Mr. Lawrence." He made a bow.

The Deco Room was a faithful recreation of a mid-thirties' nightclub, with chrome furniture and amber floor lamps arranged on a geometric-patterned carpet, with an overall effect of simple elegance. On the far side of the room a large band played the final bars of "Make Believe Ballroom," then without pausing, switched to the slower beat of "Whispering."

On the dance floor, Kurt's strong, muscular arms held Margo tightly. His hand slid appreciatively over the slim but curvaceous figure her evening gown revealed, and she rippled like a cat having its back stroked. She felt his body move in unison with hers as he maneuvered her adroitly around the floor.

She marveled at his taut, lean body and his wide, powerful shoulders, as solid as the Rock of Gibraltar. He danced expertly with the grace of a wild animal and the control of an athlete. She was Cinderella in a fabulous cloud of mist, borne along by a fantasy Prince Charming. But she knew this was no fantasy.

"I shouldn't be dancing with you," she murmured. "You're the enemy."

"I don't have to be," he said.

"Yes, you're the enemy and I'm a traitor," she said. "I should be punished for treason." ·

"Nobody's going to punish you," Kurt assured her. He guided her gently across the floor, closer to the band. For a few seconds, the volume of the music stopped any conversation as they moved together to the slow, melodious beat. When he had whirled her far enough away from the stage, she looked up at him.

"Don't think that because I'm letting you dance with me, I'll give in to you about the store. I won't."

"No?" An amused twinkle was back in his eyes.

"No," she replied matter-of-factly. "Although you *are* the handsomest enemy I've ever done a two-step with...."

"I tango, too," he offered.

"Doesn't make any difference."

"I think it does." His dark eyes seemed to bore into her soul, arousing emotions she had forced herself to hold in check. "Something's happening between us," he said, his voice suddenly husky. "And it's going to be difficult to stay on opposite sides of the fence."

Margo returned his look, but sadly, thinking that he didn't know that this was as close as they would ever get. She knew David's wounds to her emotions had made her incapable of giving in to her feelings. As the music changed, their footsteps kept pace. "It *can't* happen between us..." she began.

"It already has," Kurt said decisively. "Before you dumped fettuccine on me, before we had lunch—the second you jumped into my lap and I kissed you."

"If you say something silly like 'this is bigger than both of us,'" Margo said with a half smile, "I'll step on your toes."

Margo couldn't divine what lay behind Kurt's dark eyes. He was sizing her up, as if coming to a decision, wanting to say something, but holding back. It was clear that he wanted her, but, Margo realized, he didn't take into account their opposing business positions.

It had been a long day but an eventful one, she mused as they headed out of the restaurant a little later. A possibly long-term lunch disaster had been saved by a wound-healing evening, and perhaps there wouldn't be any regrets after today. Despite her jumpiness about men, Margo had to admit she felt strangely relaxed in Kurt's strong arms. Maybe it was enough to know that they had enjoyed the evening together. Tomorrow would probably find them fighting again—tooth and nail—on the video battleground, but she preferred to wait for that eventuality.

When they reached the door of her hotel room, Margo started to open her small clutch purse, but Kurt deftly slipped it from her hands, rummaged in it until he found the key, and pulling it out, slid the bag back under her arm.

"It's pumpkin time, Cinderella," he said tenderly.

Margo smiled. "Thank you for dinner—and the dances. I suppose after tonight I should forgive you for trying to run me out of business," she said contritely. "Are we even now?"

"There's just one more thing..." Kurt said seriously.

Margo frowned, puzzled.

"Our little duet this morning was awfully quick. I think we should have a chance to do it right."

He lowered his head and found her lips with a single smooth motion, drawing her body against his with fierce possessiveness. The searing brand of his mouth burned a path that seemed to go straight to her soul.

Margo had thought the unexpected kiss he'd given her that morning had been a fireworks display—until now. Nothing this spectacular had ever happened to her. His lips were warm, hard and insistent, forcing hers open so that he could probe the secret recesses of her mouth, his breath tasting of fine wine and fresh moistness, the sheer masculine strength of his big body dissolving her with its powerful passion.

For an instant she tried to struggle, confused by the willing response her body seemed ready to give, only to find herself trapped in his arms, snuggled against him so tightly she could hardly breathe. Whichever way she turned her face, he'd move faster, his mouth always poised for another sensuous taste of her sweet lips.

She seemed to have rubber bands for legs, and they began to tremble as his provocative, intimate kisses fanned a fire inside her that was hotter than any furnace. Her heart was running on fast forward, jumping frantically, as she tried desperately to identify the strange longings and sizzling ache deep within her body. There was something disturbing in her response, something dangerous—something that hinted at David. Had she fallen into another male trap? Suddenly frightened, she stiffened, but he only held her tighter and kept kissing her.

He plunged his fingers into her hair, controlling the tilt of her head with strong, warm pressure as he turned her face gently to meet his. His mouth pressed insistently against hers, opening slightly, tantalizing her with his provocative tongue. Under the sensual force of such an intimate attack, all resistance left her tensed body with a tiny sigh and like a sleepwalker, she began to relax.

Instinctively she obeyed his silent orders, her body alive with a new, unfamiliar passion. Her fingers spread over his broad shoulders, caressing the rock-hard muscle and blazing strength beneath the fabric. She wanted to touch those muscles, run her hand over his lean, flat belly, to live every hard line of him. God, she hadn't felt this with David—with him it had been Dick and Jane. This was Tarzan and Jane.

In a haze, she realized it was over. His lips brushed the silky tenderness of her cheek, and he looked down gently into her hazel eyes. He was smiling ever so slightly, and she wondered if he could feel her heart beating like a manic jackhammer in her chest. Did he know that her trembling was more from panic than from...? A silent, questioning look passed between them, tense and precipitous. Margo broke the spell reluctantly as he released her from his covetous arms.

"I'd better go in...." she suggested softly, turning away from him. As Kurt unlocked the door for her, pushing it wide into the room, Margo stepped in and then turned, pulling the door partially closed so that only her head was in the opening. When Kurt pressed the key back into her hand and its warmth travelled up her arm, she vowed she'd keep the key for the rest of her life. The hotel could get another one.

Margo smiled. "Good night, Kurt."

Kurt didn't reply. Instead he gently drew the back of his fingers along her smooth cheek, then reached to pull the door closed.

Chapter Four

Margo's gaze carefully swept the early-morning patrons of the coffee shop as she stood by the Please Wait to Be Seated sign just inside the entrance from the hotel lobby. Since she knew David never showed his face before nine in the morning, she'd decided a quick cup of coffee at a quarter to eight would leave her plenty of time to avoid him.

She breathed a silent sigh of relief. No sign of him. She would be able to drink her coffee in peace and go over the seminar notebook she cradled in her arm.

The heavyset waitress approached expectantly.

"No table," Margo advised. "The counter will be—"

She felt a tender touch on her upper arm and a warm brush on her cheek that made her freeze in anticipation. It couldn't be—

"Table for two," Kurt said behind her.

She turned, and her face brightened. "Kurt..." she managed in surprise.

He was dressed in a dark suit, every inch the businessman. "I've been waiting for you to show yourself. My treat."

They were shown to a table near one of the wide windows. The coffee shop was on the ground floor of the hotel, providing a view across the landscaped parking lot to the ever-hectic crush of airport traffic on Century Boulevard. After a quick perusal of the menu, they both ordered only coffee.

As soon as the waitress had left, Kurt rested his elbows easily on the tabletop and leaned forward with a friendly air.

"I see Cinderella didn't turn into a pumpkin."

"It was her coach that turned into a pumpkin," Margo pointed out. "And if you'd ever seen my poor VW bug, you'd think there'd never been a change."

Conversation halted as the waitress returned with their coffee. As Margo stirred a dollop of cream into her ceramic cup, she was conscious of Kurt's attentive gaze.

"Can I happily assume that your change in wardrobe has something to do with last night?" he asked, taking a tentative sip from his cup.

Margo's eyes flicked down over today's attire. She had chosen a white skirt and a red, tropical-print blouse instead of her mousy gray business suit. She realized he was right: not only was the outfit bright and casual, it reflected her present state of mind better than drab woolens.

Margo allowed herself a half smile and looked up from her coffee into his dark eyes. "I had a wonderful time last night. Thank you. It was a nice way to end a day that—well, could have ended very badly.''

''No day could go wrong that starts with the woman of your dreams jumping in your lap.'' Kurt's smile matched her own. ''By the way, did David and Jo have a good time at the play last night?''

''Oh, yes,'' Margo began brightly. ''Jo had never seen *South Pacific*, and David needed company—'' She stopped in midsentence, feeling a look of utter surprise come to her face. ''But how did you—?''

Kurt leaned forward conspiratorially. ''You forget—I was in the booth behind you.'' The wicked grin he displayed was proof that he was enjoying himself.

Margo was sure her face matched the crimson of her blouse. She had failed last night to put two and two together. Kurt must have heard her entire argument with David.

''Well,'' she managed, ''they had a good time, anyway.''

''Not nearly as good a time as we did, I'll bet.'' His hand found hers across the tabletop, lifting it from its position on her seminar notebook. ''We could skip the lectures today, as well.''

Margo's eyes widened as the pressure of his hand on hers resurrected the wonderful sensation she'd felt last night. What could he have on his mind this morning? It wasn't even eight o'clock yet.

''Kurt, I couldn't just leave,'' she said, shaking her head. ''I paid good money for this seminar. You may not need the information they're giving out, but I do. You forget, I have a store to run.''

''I haven't forgotten. I just thought it would be nice for us to spend a little more time with each other.''

Margo was quiet for a second as his eyes probed deep into her, willing her to accept his enticing suggestion. "There's nothing I'd like more, Kurt. Really."

"Then why not?" he prodded gently. "It'll be fun— I guarantee it."

She smiled pleasantly, trying to distance herself from him. "Oh, I believe you. It *is* fun being with you. It's just that—"

"If you say 'business before pleasure...'" Kurt threatened with a grin, leaving the sentence unfinished.

Margo laughed in spite of herself. She had indeed intended to use the timeworn cliché. Instead, she said, "The store is important to me, Kurt. I'm here to make myself into the sort of businesswoman it takes to run a store like Video Matinee. I have to think of it first."

His gaze slid to the window and he studied the crush of traffic on Century Boulevard for what seemed a long time. Finally, when he turned back, she caught a different look in his eye. She had never seen him quite so thoughtful and concerned, and she wondered what it portended.

"You'll be going home after the final lectures this afternoon?"

Margo hadn't expected such a mundane question, and her mind had to shift gears. "Yes, Jo and I are driving back to Cielito Vista tonight."

"Jo could go home alone."

A tingle went through her. Just what was he asking?

"But, why—" she began.

"If you stay another day or two," he said softly, "it'll give us the chance to get to know each other better. Last night wasn't nearly enough time."

Margo freely admitted to herself that their delightful evening had been too short. She would like to learn as much about Kurt as he wanted to know about her, but those things took time. And she knew in her heart that that time could not be now. Not when Video Matinee was so important—and especially not when he had an interest in the store, as well.

His fingers wound even closer around hers. Morning coffee had long been forgotten. "I know a little place down in San Diego," he suggested. "Beautiful. And private. Lots of shimmering sands, a lazy sun setting over sailboat masts in the bay." His gaze caught her in a languid, persuasive hold. "Quiet, romantic dinners for two overlooking the ocean—things like that were meant for you."

Margo caught her breath, not sure how to respond. The thought of running off to a seaside paradise with Kurt was tempting, and maybe that was what finally caused the warning bells to ring in her head. She couldn't deny that she liked him, and the prospect of spending undiluted hours—days—with him was enticing. But was that what he wanted? Or was this merely a clever power play?

Margo's internal security system began to erect a strong barrier, no matter how much she would have liked to knock it down. She couldn't forget what his prime purpose had been only yesterday morning: to buy Video Matinee. If it had been anyone else, she might have said yes, but with that corporate cloud hovering in the background, she had to use every ounce of willpower to resist temptation.

"Kurt, what are you saying!" She knew it was a weak reply to the torrent of indecision raging in her head, but it was the best she could do. To any ear, her exclamation might have sounded like a display of insulted dignity or a cry of joy. "I couldn't..." she stammered. "Video Matinee needs me."

Kurt's look intensified as his expressive right eyebrow rose, making him even more difficult to resist. His voice was wicked and inviting. "Do you really expect me to believe that you would be happier falling asleep during a boring lecture on videocassette sell-through than helping me sail a skiff around Mission Bay?"

Margo's heart wanted to give in. The visions he promised sounded marvelous, but she couldn't surrender. "Kurt..." She tried to keep a pleading tone out of her voice.

Kurt's fantasy spinning didn't stop. He continued, his spellbinding drawing her closer and closer to the precipice. "And the dubious honor of receiving a certificate of completion for this seminar isn't nearly as thrilling as horseback riding for two along the beach."

She couldn't let him go on. Margo had to stop this siren song before her romantic nature took possession of her.

"Kurt, stop," she said quickly. Her brisk tone masked the struggle she felt inside, and her words were slow and deliberate. "I can't. Don't you see that? Video Matinee means everything to me. I can't run off and leave it like an abandoned child—it needs me."

"What about you?" he asked tenderly, bringing the back of her hand up to his smooth, hard jaw. That one gesture, that single touch—it was almost enough to make her accept. "What do *you* need? You have to come first sometime and let the store take care of itself."

"Kurt, I *am* the store." How could she make him understand that? The romantic notions she harbored had to take second place to Video Matinee. The struggle inside her ended and her strongest instinct won. She had a commitment and it remained unchangeable.

She gently drew their joined hands away from his face and cupped his on the table. "I understand why you asked me, and I thank you for the opportunity, but I think you know that Video Matinee is the most important thing in my life."

Their eyes were locked for a few moments in a deep communion. Margo had tried to express how much she meant what she said, and she hoped he would accept her decision. His eyes were sensitive brown windows on his soul, and she saw them turn from dull disappointment to the amused glint she knew so well.

"One last chance," he chided. "Walks along the wharf at dawn...?"

Margo sighed in exasperation. "What can I say to make you understand? We both have businesses to run, or at least I assume *you* do. You seem more interested in going to San Diego than in taking care of Hot Circuit Video. Well, fine—you go to Sea World and *I'll* look after your store," she said with finality.

He was studying her again in a way that unnerved her, and she knew she had to escape or she'd be seduced by his romantic yarn spinning. She didn't know how long she could go on refusing his offer or, indeed, if she would be able to refuse it at all in the end.

Their hands parted as she made a great show of checking her wristwatch and picking up her seminar notebook. "Look at the time. It's nearly eight-thirty." Kurt was strangely silent. "I'd better get up to the room and see if Jo is ready yet. She got in way after I did last night." She was silent for a minute, not really knowing how to say what she wanted to say. "I guess I won't see you again today—the seminar's nearly over."

"It wouldn't be difficult to arrange for us to sit together..."

"Kurt," Margo said firmly, but softly, "I have a store to think about. And so do you. Maybe you should remember that."

As Margo dug in her shoulder bag for change to pay the waitress, she stood up. Kurt rose and stopped her, shutting her purse.

"I said my treat and I meant it." He leaned down and gave her a light kiss on the cheek. "I take pride in being someone who holds to his word."

"Good," Margo replied in the same sober spirit, "because so do I."

She turned briskly, heading for the exit into the lobby. Kurt caught up to her as she stepped over the threshold.

"Can I quote you on that?" That glint was back in his eyes, and Margo was relieved. She smiled, glad to play along again.

"You can carve it in granite, if you want." A lingering look passed between them. Simple words didn't seem to be enough, but they were all she had. "I'll see you, Kurt."

Kurt gave her a wink. "Sooner than you think, Margo. When you least expect it," he warned, "expect me to pop up."

Reluctantly, she left him there in the doorway to the coffee shop, wishing that, for once in her life, she didn't have the determination to see that her store was safe, and that she had been able to give in to that tantalizing amalgam of salt-and-pepper hair, those twinkling dark eyes, that expressive right eyebrow and that devastating charm.

As she stepped out of the elevator on the nineteenth floor Margo turned right, heading for the room she shared with her manager. She hadn't gone far when she noticed Jo standing out in the hall.

Jo was leaning against the doorjamb of their room, arms crossed, with an ominous cast to her features. The door was closed.

"Jo," Margo said with concern. "What's wrong? Did you lock yourself out of the room?"

"No, I didn't lock myself out of the room."

"Well, then, what—?"

Jo sighed deeply, a puzzled expression on her angular face. "Would you mind telling me just what happened last night?"

Margo felt a chill run up her spine. She hadn't revealed a word of her evening with Kurt Lawrence to her manager. "Jo," she said sternly, "nothing happened last night." She pushed past Jo, turning the doorknob. "And when I say nothing—I mean it. I swear to you...."

She opened the door and walked in, then halted immediately.

The dresser and desk were covered with vases of white, red and pink long-stemmed roses. Margo wandered into the center of the room, overcome with the sweet smell of the bouquets, while Jo came in and closed the door, leaning against the foyer wall.

Dazed, Margo stammered, "J-Jo, wh-what's this all about?"

Jo uncrossed her arms and pulled a small white envelope from the pocket of her designer jeans.

"The infamous note!" she said with mock intrigue in her voice, handing the envelope to Margo and returning to her position in the foyer, the picture of judicial curiosity.

Opening the envelope, Margo extracted the tiny florist's card inside and read it silently: "Many thanks for a truly wonderful evening. I've always liked happy endings. Kurt"

"Nothing happened last night—I swear it," Jo mimicked. "Ha! If you believe that, I have a bridge in Manhattan I want to sell you..."

Margo sat down on the bed as if she'd been forced there, her eyes open wide, her mouth agape with words she couldn't say. Jo remained unmovable, the question mark on her face patiently demanding some kind of explanation.

Margo swallowed. Fortunately, the seminar schedule was on her side, and she had no time to provide her manager with an answer. The last lecture was about to start. Jo could talk to her when they got home to Cielito Vista, and she could think of something to say.

The final seminar was long and the speaker equally long-winded. Much as Margo wanted to pay attention, she couldn't help casting a hopeful glance around the hall but Kurt wasn't in sight, and she didn't see him afterward or when she and Jo checked out of the hotel. Even so, deep down, she'd still harbored a feeling of crazy anticipation. He had said when she least expected it....

Margo watched the large brown United Parcel truck rumble away. Carefully arranging the four shoe-box-size containers he had delivered into an easily carried pile, she started for the main desk in the middle of the store.

"It's showtime!" Margo called, using the familiar Video Matinee battle cry for whenever deliveries were made. She detoured around a display of science fiction titles jutting out into the main aisle of the shop.

The design of Video Matinee was simple. At the front desk in the center of the store, rows and rows of sturdy wood-finished drawers contained the actual movies in plastic cases. The rest of the floor space was occupied by wall and floor units displaying empty videocassette covers that customers brought to the front desk and exchanged for movies of their choice. Near the back of the store, one large corner was partitioned off, and served as the stockroom where shipments were checked in and supplies stored. The store's basic colors of blue, brown and white created an overall airy, spacious effect that made Margo proud.

Margo and Jo had been back from the convention for over a week and had taken back the reins of Video Matinee from their temporary help, Bobbie and Shawna. They were pleased that everything had been handled without the slightest hitch, although business had been modest over the three-day weekend they'd been absent.

There were no customers in the store at that moment. Margo knew that Wednesday mornings were always a little slow, but nothing like this, and the lackluster business worried her. This was exactly what she'd been afraid of when the large chains began to invade the town. So far, only one VideoDynamo outlet had moved into the area, but already it seemed to have cut into her business.

Margo placed the boxes on the front desk near the cash register, reaching for the small razor knife on the shelf under the cash drawer as Jo wandered over from the New Releases section, abandoning the never-ending task of putting returned boxes on the shelf.

"Is it the new Clint Eastwood?" Jo asked eagerly as Margo slit the packing slip envelope on the side of the first box.

She drew out the yellow packing slip and unfolded it, shaking her head. "Sorry—it's a Disney."

Jo shrugged. "*Dirty Harry* or *Bambi*—I'm not picky. I see we got those classics you ordered."

Margo smiled as she opened the next packing slip. "A couple of MGM musicals. I'd better check these into stock while we're slow."

Jo nodded her understanding: the sooner the movies were checked in, the sooner they could be on the shelf. Margo bundled the boxes for easy carrying and started out of the desk area toward the partitioned workroom.

"Let me know when the mail gets here," she called back over her shoulder. "We're expecting a credit slip for those movies they sent us last month that we didn't order."

She heard Jo's shouted "Okay" as she pushed the swinging door to the supply room open with her shoulder and passed through it, letting the panel swivel closed after her.

After depositing the boxes on the long, waist-high workbench, she set to work slitting them open and stacking their contents in a neat pile to the side. As she reached for a pen in its holder to verify the packing slips, she carefully moved the green ceramic vase full of roses to the side, stopping as she did so to look again at the tall, fragrant blooms.

"Many thanks for a truly wonderful evening," she said absently under her breath.

The handwritten card lay in the top drawer of the desk in the workroom. Mixed with books of deposit slips and rubber stamps, it was hidden at the back of a small box of Video Matinee business cards. In the ten days since the seminar, Margo had more than once caught herself absently pulling the drawer open and flipping to the last card in the box. The flowers that had cascaded around their hotel room, one slightly-the-worse-for-wear vase of which now graced the workbench, were a pleasant reminder of Kurt.

She had already begun to miss him, and whatever she may have felt at the time, she regretted now that she hadn't allowed him to talk her into going to San Diego. After leaving him at the entrance of the hotel coffee shop, she hadn't seen him again, and for the past week and a half had felt bereft of his wry remarks and casual banter.

She'd never met a man with the strong physical presence and casual sensuality that Kurt Lawrence paraded so well. No other man had the power to raise goose bumps on her flesh with nothing more than an intense, honest gaze. She shivered at the memory, and realized she liked the feeling. Kurt Lawrence was man enough to be gentle and warm yet never lost firm command of the situation. Normally, his take-charge traits would have set her teeth on edge, but for some reason he stayed in her mind, teasing her with memories of lunch—a good-night kiss . . . and a sultry charisma that turned her to mush.

Margo tried to convince herself that resisting the urge to run away with him had been the right thing to do, but she'd begun to wonder. Ever since, she had gone about the motions of running Video Matinee on automatic pilot, constantly turning over the irritating question, "What if...?".

Margo continued to slit the wrappers on the video-cassettes, transferring their contents to clear plastic cases after affixing magnetic security labels to them to protect them from theft. As she stuffed the empty boxes with precut Styrofoam wedges, rewrapping them in clear plastic for display, a memory made her smile: Jo's reactions on the long drive back up the Pacific Coast after the seminars, which had been as she'd expected.

"I didn't mean to come down so hard on you," Jo had said after half an hour's silence, broken only by the car's hum.

"That's all right," Margo had assured her from behind the wheel. "I know you're worried about what might happen to the store if I associate with Kurt Lawrence."

Jo was quiet past three exits, then said, "I'm more concerned for *you*."

"Me?" Margo asked, puzzled. "But why? I'm perfectly capable...."

"And so is he," her manager put in with gentle firmness. "Margo, I worry about you as if you were my own sister."

Margo maneuvered her light blue VW Bug around a motor home and sped past it. "You're closer than a sister. If I didn't already have a mother, I'd give you the job."

"No, thank you," Jo observed wryly from the passenger seat. "I prefer wearing sandals to orthopedic oxfords." She became serious again. "I mean it, Margo. You have to admit, you haven't had much luck with men so far."

"I hope you don't count David," Margo said, slowing to pace herself with the traffic on the freeway. "He isn't a man—he's a male bulldozer."

Jo squirmed in her seat to look directly at Margo. "I *do* count David. There's been your dad, David and an unnatural attachment to Clark Gable and Tom Selleck. Your father and the last two aside, you're batting zero."

"I didn't realize you were keeping a scorecard," Margo observed ruefully.

Jo ignored the remark. "I know you got carried away with Kurt Lawrence. No one's ever been able to stop you from doing anything you put your mind to. But listen to me, Margo—not as a business partner but as a friend: please be careful. I know what you've been through with David, and I don't want to see you tear yourself apart again."

Margo deftly changed lanes, avoiding an advancing semi. "Don't you think I know better?"

"Sometimes I wonder," Jo said simply. "Since David, you've been afraid to look for Mr. Right. If you want to know the truth, I think you're headed in the same direction with the Video King. You're ripe to be swept off your feet."

"I'm afraid you're a little late, Jo," she said wistfully. "But don't worry. Unless we sign up for another seminar or rent a movie in one of his stores, I probably won't see him again."

"I said it a long time ago, but you didn't listen: if you need me, I'm here."

Margo wanted to respond to Jo's generous display of concern, but she saw their exit coming up swiftly on the right. They careened across two lanes of honking early-evening traffic to avoid missing the turnoff for Cielito Vista.

She turned to thank Jo for her support and found her manager as white as a sheet, clutching the handrail above the VW's glove compartment.

"I take it back," Jo said, wide-eyed. "If you keep on driving like that, neither one of us will be around to give *or* take any advice!"

Margo felt secure back in her tree-shaded hometown, like Andy Hardy on the cozy back lot at MGM. Cielito Vista's neat little streets and homey, small-town atmosphere were always there when she needed to retreat from too much indulgence in big cities, like the madhouse of Los Angeles. It was here that she felt safest.

Her eyes focused on the videocassette boxes in her hand, and she realized she'd mechanically wrapped two of the display boxes together. As she slit the covering plastic with a swift motion and rewrapped them separately, Jo called her name from out on the floor.

"Mail's in?" Margo asked expectantly.

Jo's voice hesitated before she answered, "Well, yeah, I suppose you could say that. You'd better get out here."

Mystified, Margo gathered up the empty boxes and cassettes and backed out the swinging door. She couldn't really see where she was headed over the pile of merchandise, but familiar landmarks in the store were enough to guide her to the front counter.

Jo, she could see from the side, was coming around the counter after helping a customer on the floor.

"What's up?" Margo asked. "Where's the mail?"

"Need some help with those?"

Every muscle in her body stiffened with shock, and a warm, glorious tide of anticipation flowed through her as she looked down and saw goose bumps rise on her arms. It was Kurt's voice—she'd know it anywhere—that thrilling baritone with its wicked sensual power was almost enough to make her collapse. She threw a desperate look at Jo, who wore an I-had-nothing-to-do-with-it expression.

"Kurt...?" Margo asked tentatively, remembering his goodbye. When you least expect it...

She peered around the pile of boxes and nearly dropped them all. The sight of Kurt, smiling and swarthy, his elbows propped casually on the counter, was like a blow to the stomach. Margo breathed a speechless sigh of astonishment, feeling a familiar tingle run through her body. She stared. And stared. She didn't try to hide the absurd little smile that crept to her lips.

"Hi, beautiful," he smiled. "Let me give you a hand."

Chapter Five

Kurt suited action to words and relieved Margo of her burden, setting the videocassettes and boxes on the counter. He was dressed casually in a black tropical print shirt, open at the throat, that clung suggestively to the muscles across his chest and to his biceps. A loose pair of white cotton pants encased his powerful legs. He was a sight for sore eyes, Margo thought. And for healthy ones, too.

"I thought I'd never see you again," she gasped. Out of the corner of her eye, she spotted Jo hovering nearby, an expression of unveiled wariness on her mobile face, and quickly changed her tune. "I mean, what are you doing here?"

He leaned across the counter and cupped his hand against his mouth, close to her ear. "I couldn't live without you," he whispered, then straightened up with a wink.

Margo could hardly contain herself. His arrival was like the answer to a prayer. Suddenly, she ran her fingers through her blond hair, dragging it back, away from her face, and looked down mournfully at the blue jumpsuit she had on.

"Kurt, I must look a mess...."

"Nonsense," he said. "I said 'hello, beautiful,' and I meant it."

Jo snorted and came forward.

"I think I'd better get these on the floor," she said matter-of-factly, scooping the pile of empty videocassette boxes into her arms. "Don't mind me," she threw over her shoulder pointedly as she moved away, casting a wary glance at Kurt.

Kurt watched with amusement as Jo moved out onto the floor and then returned his attention to Margo. "I hope I haven't come at an inopportune moment."

Margo drew closer, so that their conversation would be private. "Oh, don't mind Jo. She's playing Juliet's nurse." Then she got down to the basics. "What are you doing here?" she asked again.

"Oh, I was just passing through town...." he began easily.

Margo waved his remark away with her hand. "Don't give me that. I can't imagine you just 'passing through' anywhere. Tell the truth and say that you came up here to see me."

"As a matter of fact, I did."

Margo felt a comforting warmth just being with him and talking to him again. Now that he was actually here, every morose thought that had been in her head for the past few days departed.

"I've missed you," she confessed.

"Life hasn't exactly been the same without you, either." The affectionate look in his eyes was heaven.

He cast a wary glance around the interior of the store. Business was slow, with only two customers among the display shelves. Jo was moving industriously around the floor, pausing occasionally to peer suspiciously over the top of the display rack at the twosome at the front counter.

"Is there somewhere we can go and talk?" he asked, turning to fix her with his deep brown eyes.

"Well," Margo managed, "there's the workroom, but—"

"Somewhere private," he stressed. "And out of the way. On the way into town, I saw kind of a fishing village at the beach." His smile was back. "I have a surprise for you." He punctuated this by touching her nose gently with his index finger.

Margo was at a loss for words. She couldn't leave Jo to mind the store alone—that would be unfair. In another ten minutes, though, Bobbie Hamilton, one of her part-time help, would arrive. Then she could escape with ease. She explained the situation to Kurt and he agreed.

When Bobbie was five minutes early, Margo thanked whatever guardian angel was making things go right for her today. Grabbing her bag from under the counter and slipping the strap over her shoulder, she told Kurt she was ready to go. As she came out from behind the counter, Jo approached.

"Jumping ship?" she asked wryly.

"Only for a little while," Margo advised her. "I won't be gone long."

Her manager accepted this vague information. "Just stay out of Italian restaurants—at least those that serve fettuccine."

Margo turned crimson at the memory of the last time she had been spirited away by Kurt with no explanation, but he beat her to a reply.

"That's okay," he said reassuringly. "She knows who I am this time."

Outside, he settled Margo in his white Mercedes sedan and took his place on the crushed gold velour of the driver's seat. The Mercedes' engine came to life with a humming surge as Kurt revved it, then slipped it into gear.

Three blocks from the store, Margo suggested a right turn onto Faulkner Place and he complied immediately. She peered through the windshield alertly, for they were nearing the spot—*her* spot. She recognized the California-Spanish tile roof of the sprawling ValuMart shopping plaza coming up on their right.

"Slow down," she advised.

Because traffic was light, Kurt had no problem doing so. "What is it?"

Margo pointed to a large vacant lot on the left side of the street, directly across from the enormous Spanish-style shopping mall. "See that? That's the historic site of a dream. *My* dream to be specific."

"Ah." Kurt nodded in quick understanding. "The future home of the vast Video Matinee empire." He studied the lot with interest as they crawled past it.

"The same," she assured him. "I believe that if you want something badly enough," she said thoughtfully, "then you eventually find a way of getting it."

Traffic became heavier and Kurt was forced to speed up, leaving the site of Margo's dream-store-to-be behind them as he followed her directions to the beach.

Mariner's Village, on the edge of Cielito Vista Bay, was a large conglomeration of New England-style clapboard buildings housing a variety of specialty shops with a weathered boardwalk running its length. A wide stretch of golden sand was the only thing between the row of shops and the royal blue of the Pacific. Kurt easily found a space in the parking lot, and soon he and Margo were sauntering down the boardwalk.

Margo paused across from Fishy Threads, a shop selling nautical clothing, and leaned on the railing. The spicy scent of the sea, less than a hundred yards away, floated to them on the mild breeze.

"You said you wanted to talk to me," she reminded him.

She knew it had to be something important or he wouldn't have gone to such lengths to ensure privacy for their conversation. The thought of San Diego and his promise of candlelit dinners and horseback riding came to her mind immediately—was he going to broach the subject again?

He stood next to her, leaning on the weathered railing, watching the ocean slide onto the warm sand in gentle, foamy rolls. "I don't really know how to begin."

She watched as the sea breeze tousled his carefully combed hair and smiled inwardly, thinking that it gave him a little-boy look. She admitted to herself that she had never felt quite this way about anyone. Standing here in the bright Southern California sun, being close to him again—near enough to touch—kindled a warmth in the pit of her stomach that made her question her own emotions.

Again the thought of San Diego entered her mind. She wanted to be with him, learn about him, and the only way to do that was by giving in to temptation. Kurt had been right: she needed to think about herself once in a while.

"Kurt," she began, "if it's about San Diego—"

He shook his head. "It isn't about San Diego." He turned and looked at her from the fathomless depths of his eyes. She saw a muscle in his jaw move ever so slightly, as if the words he wanted to say could no longer be contained.

"Hot Circuit Video is in trouble," he said evenly, without emotion.

This was the last thing Margo expected and the subject surprised her. "The whole chain?"

"It could be. I have a classic case of one bad store that's capable of bringing down the whole operation."

"But with you, with your corporate expertise, running the whole thing..."

"From the impression you got of my stores and from their sinking returns, I think it's pretty obvious that I haven't been running the stores the way I should have been. In fact, I haven't been running them at all."

Margo's brows drew together in a puzzled frown. "But then who...?"

"I don't think I told you about my younger brother, Mike. He's a good kid—about your age. About a year ago I turned Hot Circuit Video over to him."

"Very generous of you," Margo commented.

"Mike studied business in college, but when he got out, that oh-so-important piece of academic paper called a degree didn't mean much when it came to finding employment. He needed a job and I gave it to him. He wanted a chance and I felt I owed him that much."

Margo nodded.

"I thought he was a godsend, really, because a lot was happening about that time. My company, Lawrence, Limited, had just diversified into other products. You've heard of Bonnie Lee Pastries?"

Margo smiled in recognition. "You're Bonnie Lee?"

"The same." Kurt's face showed no amusement.

"You don't look at all like the pictures on the boxes—" Margo quipped, thinking of the grandmotherly portrait that graced the blue and white striped boxes of Bonnie Lee Pastries. "You're much more matronly in print."

"So I've been told. Anyway, I had my hands full. There's a hell of a lot of work in getting something like that off the ground. On top of all that, my father died."

Margo's face fell in concern. "Oh, Kurt, I'm sorry. I didn't know."

"We'd expected it," Kurt said philosophically. "He'd had two heart attacks already and they'd sort of prepared all of us, including Dad. But when he died, I came into control of his construction firm. Suddenly, I found myself in the business of putting up hotels. Of course, my Uncle John did what he could to help."

"The same uncle who set you up in the video business?" Margo asked, recalling a conversation they'd had in Los Angeles.

Kurt nodded. "He gave me his best men to help whip Lawrence, Limited, into shape. I was up to my armpits in contracts and bids and advertising for Bonnie Lee—you name it. That's when I thought of Mike. Hot Circuit was a well-oiled machine, so I let him take it over. He needed the experience, and I needed the time to devote to the rest of the growing corporation. I really thought I was doing the right thing."

Margo was fully involved now. She could envision Kurt so wrapped up in the explosion of his corporate empire that he had little and then no time to worry about Hot Circuit Video. "But what went wrong?"

Kurt stared out at the rolling surf. "I went wrong—from the start. Even though he's a great kid, Mike's always been kind of wild. Hell, he went to Europe one summer in high school and ended up in a Paris jail for helping some radicals picket the president's palace. He didn't even know what he was picketing!" Margo thought a nostalgic smile passed over Kurt's face, but it was gone in a second. "I thought four years of college had tamed him—I mean, I thought I knew my own brother. I brought him into the Hot Circuit circle and guided him around for a couple of months and then left him in charge."

A hard cast came over Kurt's features. "About a month ago I finally had everything in order with the hotel construction and Bonnie Lee, and was actually able to sit down and see how Mike was doing. Believe me, I wasn't prepared for what I saw."

"What was he picketing this time?" Margo asked, attempting to inject a little levity into the narrative for Kurt's sake.

"He wasn't picketing anything—in fact, he wasn't doing a damned thing. There hadn't been an active Hot Circuit franchise drive in months, profits had begun to slip—not an enormous amount, but enough for someone to take notice. Theft in the stores was astronomical because security was practically nonexistent. When I found out, I blew up. He'd been using Hot Circuit Video as a plaything."

"What did you do?"

Kurt was silent, struggling with something inside him that was obviously very unpleasant. "I fired him," he said simply.

"Oh, Kurt," Margo gasped. "You didn't."

"I had to," he shrugged, the look on his face an appeal for understanding. "I just told him 'That's it, you had your chance. I've been generous to a fault, but even my generosity runs out.' I didn't want to do it, but I had to." He saw Margo giving him a slightly incredulous look. "I didn't throw him out in the street, if that's what you're thinking. I had a long talk with Uncle John and he agreed to help. Mike's working for him in Santa Barbara where he can keep an eye on him."

"Well," Margo sighed. "At least it isn't a bad ending, after all. You have control of Hot Circuit Video again and you're getting it back on track. I don't see why you have to blame yourself—if anything, it was Mike's doing."

"That's just what I don't want you or anyone else to think," Kurt said firmly. There was an angry edge to his voice as he continued. "I'm not trying to find any excuses for what's happened to the store and I'm not pushing any of this off on Mike's shoulders. It was my responsibility from the start: I let my own family ties influence my decision, and I have only myself to blame.''

Somehow, she knew this confession wasn't the primary purpose of their meeting. "Kurt, that isn't why you dragged me all the way out here—to unburden your conscience about your store. You said you had a surprise for me," Margo said, hoping she could provoke him into saying his piece.

''I guess there's no way except to come right out with it.'' He reached to an inside pocket of the white jacket he'd put on as they left the car, drew out a folded document at least a dozen pages in length and handed it to her.

Puzzled, Margo accepted it and unfolded it, feeling apprehensive. A chill finger traveled down her spine when she recognized the papers as a contractual agreement.

"The party of the first part, hereinafter known as Lawrence, Limited," she read as her hand began to tremble, "and the party of the second part, hereinafter known as Margo Shepard..."

A cold horror flooded her, and she felt her hands become clammy as she sensed some devious machination. She only scanned the rest of the page, noting references to Hot Circuit Video, Kurt, and herself. Finances were spelled out in a paragraph that her eyes fled from, fearful of learning the ultimate fate that was in store for Video Matinee.

Oh, my God, she thought, stunned to immobility by this ghastly revelation. My store. Not my store. He wants to take Video Matinee away from me.

Chapter Six

Margo didn't bother turning to the second page of the contract, but thrust it back at him. A wrenching pain tore through her heart as she turned to Kurt, her face now a stone mask of determination and resentment.

"I'm not selling the store to you, Kurt. You can't use my store to make up for the mistakes in your own." Her voice was choked but firm. "I may be taking a beating from the competition, but I'm not through yet." Tears blinded her eyes as she turned to stalk off.

She barely had time to notice the shocked concern on Kurt's face as he bundled her into his arms. "My God, Margo, no," he said quickly, his hand coming up to brush her windblown blond hair from her face. "I'm not after your store."

The sound of accusation underscored her words. "Then what's that piece of paper?"

Kurt pressed it back into her hands. "Read it and you'll see I have no desire to buy Video Matinee. Please," he entreated.

Kurt released her and stepped back to let her study the document in depth without his interference. Only the fluttering feeling in her heart made her look at the contract and begin reading. She had read only two long paragraphs of legalese when she looked up at him in astonishment. In very clear and precise words, they spelled out a corporate meeting of the minds.

The incredulity was impossible to keep out of her voice. "You want us to be partners?"

"You're in trouble, Margo," he said firmly. "It's a fact that smaller stores like yours will be knocked out of the running when the big guys hit town."

Margo knew the trouble she'd have and didn't particularly appreciate the fact being pressed home. She was already experiencing the effects of competition from the new VideoDynamo store on the other side of town.

"We'd make a wonderful team, Margo," he insisted. "With your creative management and my financial support and larger stores we could be the biggest thing in video since Sony."

Margo knew that, much as she hated to admit it, she could use all the help she could get. She returned her attention to the agreement. "What's this about conditions?"

"I want you to come in and overhaul my problem store from top to bottom to stop a domino effect that could ruin me."

"But, Kurt," Margo protested, trying to divine in his face an explanation of this strange turn of events, "you could do all this yourself."

"I can't do it myself. There's no time. I have more than one business now—Hot Circuit Video is going to suffer if I can't give it the serious attention it deserves."

"You could hire a professional consultant. Why bring me into it?"

"Because you have dynamic ideas, Margo," he explained. "With your talk of dream stores, marquees over the door and stores that look like lobbies in old movie theaters, you've reawakened something in me, something the corporate noose had almost strangled: creativity. The talent you have is too valuable to let slip away."

"I appreciate your asking me, but I don't really see how..."

His warm hand closed over hers. "Margo, I'm doing this for both of us, but mostly for you."

"For me?"

"You need protection...."

"You're starting to sound like David," she said, wary of what might come next.

Kurt shook his head. "I mean your store. Margo, the competition is coming. *Fierce* competition. That's the nature of our business."

Margo swallowed. His words were downright truth. He could read her business future like a book—a book she had become tired of reading. He seemed to have all the answers, and she couldn't shake the feeling that deft fingers were again steering her in a desired direction.

"With my financial backing, you could have that store you want so badly. You can have it *now* instead of somewhere down the line, and with enough profits to start that video empire of yours."

"But a partnership?" Margo questioned. A caution light went on in her head. "Then Video Matinee would be half yours. I can't, Kurt. I can't."

"I wouldn't touch Video Matinee," he assured her, reaching to turn the pages of the contract back to a particular place. "There," he pointed to a paragraph. "The store is yours and it'll stay yours. It's right there in black and white."

Yes, indeed, she thought as she read the paragraph. Video Matinee was safe in its little niche, out of Lawrence, Limited's influence. It all seemed so calculated, so tidy. She still wasn't convinced and said so.

Kurt tried to explain. "We both come out ahead in this. With my money and your creative power, we could become a major force in this business. Video is screaming for something new and exciting and I know we can answer that cry for help."

They were silent for a moment, then Kurt's voice drifted over the salt-scented air.

"Margo—let me do this for you. Please."

His words finally struck a chord, and a strange feeling deep in Margo's heart made her speechless. Kurt had just handed her the means of becoming the businesswoman she had always wanted to be and provided the solution to all her worries about Video Matinee's future. She should feel gratitude, elation— something besides the gnawing doubts in her subconscious mind.

The pressure to accept his offer was overpowering. After all, it would enable her to shape an entire aspect of the video industry and it would be her talent, her ideas that made it possible—it would be madness to refuse such an offer.

"No more nickel-and-diming about store expenses," she breathed thoughtfully.

Kurt was attentive to her every sound, drawing closer. "With my financial resources, you'd have the money to get your dream started."

Margo leaned against the railing and concentrated hard on the ocean in front of them, as if it were a mammoth motion picture screen projecting the suddenly attainable future.

She could see it all clearly. "I could order any movies I wanted, without having to worry about a budget every five minutes."

"You'd have one of the best selections in the whole area, if you wanted," Kurt promised her.

"A free hand in construction, design—everything," she mulled aloud. "Just like an artist, with my signature on each and every store." She watched that personal vision on the horizon until it was too much to resist. She paused so long before giving her answer that she was afraid he would back down. "I'll do it," she said simply. She turned to him and caught a look of intense relief in his eyes.

He brought her hand to his lips and kissed it tenderly. "You won't be sorry. I promise you that."

Exhilaration filled her at the touch of his lips on the back of her hand, and the growing realization that she was now on the threshold of her dream made her feel a little giddy. She had accepted. She wondered how other people felt when the nearly impossible goal they had worked for for so long was suddenly within arm's reach. And all she had to do was work for Kurt, renovating his store. It was as simple as that....

Her churning thoughts ground to a halt. "Wait a minute."

"What's wrong?" He looked a question.

"What about Video Matinee?"

"I thought I told you," he stressed. "It doesn't enter into this agreement at all. I'm not planning—"

"I don't mean that. What about when I'm working on your store? Jo can't possibly run the place all by herself. I need to be there."

"You have part-time help, don't you?"

"Bobbie and Shawna, yes," she confessed. "The community college let out last week and they're both available. But what an expense. At least I work for nothing sometimes."

"We can work something out to suit everybody," Kurt assured her.

"And another thing: it's an awfully long drive down to Los Angeles every day. If I'm going to commute, I'm going to have to have mileage." She waited for Kurt's response, not expecting he would balk at such a logical expense.

To her surprise, he shook his head. "Won't work." Seeing the expression on her face, he hastened to explain. "It isn't the money or anything. It's the time factor. I don't think you could commute for two hours every morning and again at night without some sort of strain."

"Well, other people do it all the time."

He remained unconvinced. "No, you'll have to stay in Los Angeles."

"But why should I stay in a hotel? It would be cheaper if you just paid me mileage."

His brow furrowed in thought before he rejected this suggestion, too. "A hotel wouldn't allow us to be in constant contact about decisions. You'd have to be available at a moment's notice, ready to go to one of the stores when I'm—you know, the only logical solution I can see is that you stay at my house."

Margo's eyes widened as an infuriatingly innocent expression appeared on Kurt's classically angular features. His expressive right eyebrow rose in eloquent punctuation.

"Move in ... with you ... ?" Margo's words came out as if spoken by a zombie. She had been prepared for just about anything but this: living in the same house, sharing the same rooms, seeing one another practically twenty-four hours a day. Who knew how long the job of renovating his stores would take? The distinct aroma of a rotten deal was getting stronger. "I—" she stammered. "I couldn't—"

"It would only be for six weeks or so," he informed her.

"Six weeks!"

"Well," he explained, "I'd want you to renovate the one store and then stick around to see the results. Shore up any little problems that might turn up. The store's in a lot of trouble."

"But living with you?" Margo's mind struck an impassable groove. "When you mentioned San Diego the other day, I almost said yes. I mean, a couple of days in a hotel, separate rooms, all the proprieties observed. But six weeks? And in the same *house*? I couldn't, Kurt. I come from a very old-fashioned family. If my mother ever found out about it, no matter how innocent I am or how hard I'm working, she would—"

The pressure of his hand on hers silenced her. "What's the difference between a hotel and a house? They both have a common roof, don't they? Margo, the place is huge—it's an old Hollywood palazzo with over twenty rooms. You'll practically have an entire wing of the house to yourself.''

''But, still—'' she protested. She didn't appreciate being put in this position. If she followed her suspicions, she could easily think that this final revelation had been the real motivation behind his surprising generosity.

''I have a housekeeper,'' Kurt told her. ''She's as efficient as a computer and as protective as a mother hen.''

''But, Kurt—''

''No 'but, Kurt' about it,'' he said firmly. ''It's the only reasonable way to go about this. I have rooms I probably haven't walked through in a year. Hell, I'm not even sure the house has twenty rooms—it might be more.''

Margo sighed in defeat, realizing that she couldn't keep her protestations up forever. Even if she did, Kurt would be able to parry each and every one of them. If the house was really that gigantic and the protective presence of his housekeeper constantly in evidence, then maybe there wouldn't be too much of a problem.

Being in close proximity to him day and night would be a distraction. A pleasant one, she admitted, but a distraction just the same. She was concerned that the quality and content of her work might be adversely affected by their provocative living arrangements, but she thought again of the glorious opportunity this was for Video Matinee's future.

Closing her eyes, Margo nodded her head wearily in a display of resigned acceptance. ''All right, all right.'' Suddenly she fixed Kurt with an even look. ''But,'' she said, emphasizing her words with her index finger like a mother chastising a child, "I want my room to be at the opposite end of the house from yours."

Kurt started to laugh and it was a relieving sound. "Anything you say," he smiled.

She leaned back on the railing with a sigh of satisfaction. "At least I can sleep easier knowing that my *mother* will sleep easier."

Margo's drive into Los Angeles four days later was uneventful. The June weather was warm, but not as stifling as it could have been. Sunday afternoon traffic was light and she made good time; the Sunset Boulevard turnoff came up sooner than expected.

Plunging into the crush of traffic on the famous thoroughfare, Margo marveled again at the amazing speed with which forces had moved to start her on the journey toward her dream. Had it really only been four days ago that she and Kurt had stood leaning against the railing of the Mariner's Village boardwalk? So short a time since the path to everything she wanted as a businesswoman had been opened in front of her?

As her lawyer, Mr. Tremaine, had read the contractual agreement outlining Kurt's proposal he had remained maddeningly silent. As Margo watched him flip through the dozen or so closely typed pages, she had the anxious feeling he would read the document and find some glaring loophole that she'd overlooked. Her fears seemed confirmed when Mr. Tremaine heaved a weary sigh and shook his head when he reached the end of the contract. Perhaps she'd been right, and it was too good to be true.

Then Mr. Tremaine had looked at her evenly, in his most serious lawyerlike way, and told her she would be a fool not to enter into the agreement. Kurt Law-rence, he assured her, had handed her the video world on a silver platter—and put it in writing. She couldn't ask for more than that. She had signed, but not with-out misgivings. Deep inside her, common sense whis-pered that anything that seemed too good to be true usually was, but she certainly couldn't put her finger on the problem here. Even though there were no visi-ble strings attached, she knew by now that Kurt Law-rence had a bag full of special effects that he used to get what he wanted.

As she entered the area of Sunset where tall hedges and thick foliage screened wide lawns and million-dollar mansions, Margo watched her surroundings keenly.

She smiled when she thought of the look on Jo's face when she had heard the news. It had been the first time in her life she had ever known Jo to be without some sort of retort, and the moment had been price-less. Margo had weathered her manager's dire warn-ings about the proposed agreement, and Jo had finally bowed to logic when confronted with the hard facts. The obvious advantages that the agreement presented for Video Matinee and Margo had won Jo over—grudgingly. It had helped that the day had been one of the worst rental days they'd ever experienced. Sud-denly, the prospect of dreams coming true had changed Jo's mind.

Margo peered up a side street and eliminated that route. Her hand-drawn map didn't show a right turn here. She was familiar with the entire area of elite homes. Many times, she had ventured out for self-conducted tours of Beverly Hills and Bel-Air, driving for hours along the snakelike streets in the hope of seeing movie stars, and taking great delight from even the smallest glimpse of a glorious superstar's home, but potluck was the best she'd ever encountered. Margo was positive she'd seen Doris Day walking her dog along Rexford Drive—at least it had looked like Doris Day.

Margo scanned the star-studded neighborhood as she carefully followed the map Kurt had drawn for her. She'd liked his idea of driving down Sunday afternoon to settle in. It would, he'd explained, give her a chance to start fresh on Monday morning. Declining his offer of a car and a driver to convey her into Los Angeles, she'd opted instead for her sputtering VW Bug, for she preferred to have her own transportation. Her own baby-blue Bug at her side was a reassuring assertion that Kurt hadn't controlled every aspect of their deal, and with her own car, at least she could come and go as she pleased.

Margo consulted the map again. After a left turn on Beverly Drive, she was soon climbing the fabled hills. The farther into the celestial neighborhood she drove, the less she saw of houses and the more she was confronted with tall stone walls and wrought-iron gates. It was obvious that people on the hill definitely wanted their privacy as Beverly turned into Coldwater Canyon Drive and the houses became even farther apart.

A rise in the one and a half lane street led to a sharp dip, and she slowed the car before an imposing grill-work of black wrought iron gates. This was it: the map stopped here. She could feel her heart beat faster beneath the light cotton cloth of her yellow peasant blouse.

She pulled up to the gates and rolled down her window. On the driver's side of the gatepost was a prominent red button and Margo reached across the short expanse to push it.

Instantly, an intercom speaker below it crackled to life. Kurt's voice, though tinny, was unmistakable.

"Margo?"

"It's me," she affirmed. The mechanical quality of his voice through the speaker made the gated entrance more imposing and ominous. What sort of machine was she confronting? "Cinderella finally made it in her German pumpkin."

She heard the sound of his mild laughter on the other end of the intercom. "Come on up. I'll open the gates."

With a raucous buzz, the gates unlatched automatically and swung slowly open. Margo gunned the motor and completed the left turn, pulling through to the base of the cobblestone driveway, and the gates closed behind her.

The closing of the tall gates had a startling finality and she swallowed a lump of nervousness in her throat. Why do I feel like Joan Fontaine in *Rebecca*? she asked herself.

A tremor passed through her, not at the memory of the vintage film, but at the realization of exactly what she was doing. She'd let herself be spirited away from the security of Cielito Vista, only to enter a literally closed world that might be either a blessing or a threat. She shook her blond head in denial of her fear. She had already decided the stay in Kurt's house was to be business—period. Whatever she felt for him had to be restrained until they were on mutually neutral ground.

The proximity of living in the same house for six weeks or so had to be put out of her mind. She'd made a vow to herself when Kurt presented the agreement that she wouldn't allow her feelings for him to affect her work, and she renewed that resolve now. As she coaxed the VW up the steep, tree-bordered incline of the drive, she kept *Rebecca* in the forefront of her mind.

"Last night," she quoted from memory, "I dreamt I went to Manderley again."

Making one more turn to the left, she knew her hazel eyes must be fairly glimmering with fascination as Kurt's fabulous mansion came into view.

Chapter Seven

Margo guided her light blue VW Bug into a circular graveled drive in front of the house and brought the car to a halt in front of the wide, half-moon steps. Her eyes widened in wonder.

The house was a magnificent, sprawling palazzo, like the ones she had seen in a book of movie stars' homes from the twenties and thirties. Its nostalgic beauty was enhanced by the crisp, gleaming white stucco which bordered rows of tall, arched windows, covered by black wrought-iron grillwork on the front of the house. Its stunning simplicity of design created a home of exquisite period flavor. The only color that intruded on the sleekness of its white facade was the gold of Spanish roof tiles. The green of slender cypress trees and low evergreen bushes enhanced the effect, and a rolling lawn surrounded the house like an emerald velvet blanket.

The massive beveled glass front doors opened. Kurt came out on the wide portico as Margo stepped from the car, openly admiring the house.

"It's beautiful!"

"It's home," he said simply. He looked casual today in gray slacks and a light blue polo shirt. Portrait of a Business Tycoon on His Day Off, Margo decided as a caption to the scene before her.

"That's like William Randolph Hearst calling San Simeon a cottage," she exclaimed.

Kurt came down the steps to the car and took Margo's hand, bringing it to his lips. "I'm glad you finally got here. I was getting worried."

She smiled up at him. "The traffic wasn't heavy. No need to worry—"

"I didn't mean the traffic," he said. "I was afraid that some last-minute thoughts would keep you away."

A look passed between them, and Margo could see the concern in his eyes. "No last-minute thoughts," Margo confessed. "Just nervousness."

"Now, that I won't stand for." Kurt released her hand and reached into the back seat of the car for her luggage. Margo took the shoulder bag he passed to her. Lifting her suitcase, he toted it onto the columned front porch, nodding for her to go ahead.

"Go on in," he urged.

Margo ventured through the ornate portal with apprehension. White and gray walls soared with precise angularity from a floor of highly polished oak-colored tile. Only a couple of tastefully selected art deco chairs and a white enamel table graced the emptiness of the foyer. To the right, a wide staircase with wrought iron banisters curved up to the second floor. Behind her,

Kurt nudged the doors closed as he brought her suitcase inside.

"Well, what do you think?" he asked with pride.

The place was beautiful, Margo had to admit, but it was a stark beauty—with a forsaken feeling that made her think of a deserted motion picture set. Even so, she mustered the only words she could think of on such short notice.

"Awfully white, isn't it?"

His eyes met hers, as if not sure whether her comment had been a joke or not, then the dubious look in his eyes disappeared. "Upstairs," he said, nodding. "I'd have Mrs. Post show you, only it's her day off."

"Mrs. Post?"

"Housekeeper. Cook. Resident watchdog of young ladies' chastity," Kurt informed her, heading for the curving staircase. "You name it."

Margo felt a sudden fear. The presence of Kurt's housekeeper had been one of the conditions of the deal, and here it was her first minute inside the house and the woman wasn't anywhere around.

"I'll look forward to meeting her," she said as she followed him toward the stairs, hoping that he would understand the emphasis in her words. "It should be interesting seeing the woman that keeps a palace like this looking so perfect."

Kurt laughed as they neared the head of the stairs. "You'd do better looking for the lost continent of Atlantis. Mrs. Post is sort of wraithlike."

Margo paid no attention to his wry comments. All she could think of was that the living arrangement with Kurt had just turned suspicious. His remarks didn't paint the same reassuring portrait they had four days ago and the specter of control floated in the air.

"You're sure you *have* a housekeeper...." She didn't bother to conceal the skepticism in her voice.

"I must have one," he commented with a shrug, reaching the top of the flight. "I pay *someone* every month. I get cancelled checks back with her signature. And somebody fixes all my meals."

This explanation was hardly mollifying, but Margo realized it was better than nothing. Still, she would be anxious to meet Mrs. Post.

Upstairs, in the hallway were the same colors, the same sparsity of furnishings. The only deviation was a muted geometric-patterned carpet laid in a perfect ribbon down the center of the gleaming tiles.

With its simple and angular style, the house was a magnificent tribute to the jazz age, but at the same time, Margo felt a lifeless chill to the place. The atmosphere was impersonal, as if no one lived in it.

Kurt stopped at a door halfway down the corridor.

"Home Sweet Away-from-Home," he announced, opening the door. He preceded her into the spacious room and hoisted her suitcase to a small upholstered stool at the base of the wide queen-size bed.

Kurt had given her more than a room; he had provided a complete suite. The thought of a hotel entered her mind, and she remembered with amusement her comments to him about the safe impersonality of hotel lodgings. He had kept his word; here she could be as completely isolated as her whim dictated.

And he had gone to great trouble to make the suite comfortable. The bedroom, furnished with warmth and care, was more welcoming than any room she had seen in the house so far. A large dresser of polished teak and walnut stood opposite a tall wardrobe, and the wide oval mirror over the dressing table reflected the room's warm wood colors. On the right, a door led, she could see, to a sparkling black and white bathroom. Through the arch at the other end of the room, she glimpsed a spacious sitting room with two overstuffed chairs, upholstered in 1930s chintz, and an antique desk with a cane-backed chair.

Kurt crossed the room to the closed burgundy curtains and pulled them back, exposing a spectacular view of the surrounding mountains through the beveled glass of French doors. On the other side of the glass was a balcony, ringed with black wrought-iron railings.

Margo settled her shoulder bag on the bed as Kurt turned away from the windows.

"I hope you like it," he said. In his eyes, Margo could see the same peculiar pride she had encountered only moments before, but this time she didn't entertain the idea of saying something noncommittal or funny.

Sensing that he must have gone to some trouble to select just the right room and furnishings for her, she appreciated his efforts to live up to his word about their living arrangements. "I think it's marvelous," she said sincerely. "Thank you."

The warm look in Kurt's eyes confirmed that he had paid particular care to seeing her demands were met. "The doors all have locks, too, in case you're worried," he said with a smile. "And I promise I'll have Mrs. Post present herself to you the minute she arrives in the morning—that is, if I can find her."

Margo laughed. "I'll look forward to it."

Kurt suggested a tour of the house and Margo eagerly accepted. For the next hour and a half they wandered through a succession of opulent rooms, with

Kurt always ready with an interesting or amusing anecdote about the various movie stars who had lived in the house decades earlier.

Theda Bara, he revealed, used to give readings of poetry in the solarium, Wallace Beery and Gloria Swanson had once spent a week in the very room she now occupied and Rudolph Valentino had whirled innumerable starlets across the terrazzo tiles in the palatial ballroom. From several windows, he pointed out the meticulously manicured gardens where more than one film-land wedding had taken place.

The estate was a veritable storybook of celluloid fairy tales about the famous and infamous of Hollywood, and Margo was enchanted from the first second. The mansion quickly lost its impersonal atmosphere. That feeling couldn't last long, Margo decided with pleasure—not in the illustrious company of the stars who were part of its grandiose past.

It was nearly seven o'clock when Kurt escorted Margo to her room and told her to dress for dinner. Twenty minutes later Margo reached the bottom of the stairs, clad in a dress of creamy white silk. She bent to slip her right foot out of its red high-heeled shoe and straightened the toe of her stocking when she heard Kurt's deep, resonant voice from a room off the hallway.

"Is that you?" Kurt asked as he appeared in the hall.

He looked elegant in his black evening clothes. The frilled front of his shirt seemed to make his already wide chest even more expansive, and the carefully tailored jacket needed no padding whatsoever; he filled it out more than admirably. His slim hips and powerful legs were encased in a pair of black dress pants with a crease that looked sharp enough to cut paper.

Kurt's chocolate-brown eyes were unabashedly admiring. His gaze swept covetously down her floor-length white gown, taking in the billowing folds of the sheer off-the-shoulder sleeves and turning back up again when he saw the tips of cherry-red shoes peeking out under the hem. Margo was fully aware of his avid scrutiny and she laughed nervously.

"Am I being invited to dinner, or am *I* dinner?"

He took her hand in his. "We'll have to see. You may be dessert."

As he propelled her across a wide room to a set of French doors leading out to the dusk-shrouded terrace beyond, he bent slightly and turned a couple of switches on an end table that contained a console. A soft Big Band tune filled the air. From there, they continued out to the terrace.

Dinner was a delicious affair. His favorite wine, duck *à l'orange*, a round table set simply and elegantly for two. The flames of two tall white candles flickered gently in a slight movement of warm early night air, and amber carriage lights at intervals along the back of the house lent a romantic ambience to the setting. The view from the flagstone terrace was marvelous: at one side rose a mountain dotted with rich homes, their lights shining brightly as night cloaked them and to the right and below them was the city of Los Angeles, turning into a fairyland of colored lights and streamers as the day's light dwindled.

Afterward, Kurt coaxed her into a slow dance to the hushed tones of Jimmy Dorsey. The lilting melodies were entrancing, and Margo felt the familiar sensations of that night weeks ago when she and Kurt had moved together around the Deco Room dance floor. She liked the clean masculine smell of him and the musky aroma of his cologne, the gentle grace of his movements and the intimate pressure of his hand on her back, holding her against his solid frame. In the dim, romantic illumination of the carriage lamps his determined features were almost irresistible, and the muted light danced in the darkness of his eyes.

Tonight she felt expansive, sure that they were on the threshold of a special venture and the evening had a certain aura of quiet celebration about it.

After the fifth circumnavigation of the terrace, Margo begged for a rest. They went to the edge of the terrace where they had left their wineglasses, and from there they could look out over the entire canyon, inky in the darkness—a velvet blackness that seemed silent and calm.

Kurt refilled her glass and then his own, setting the bottle down on the wide stone railing. "A toast," he said softly, the amber light glowing in his eyes.

Margo raised her glass. "To what?"

"To you. And what you're doing for me."

A sudden warmth spread over Margo as the rims of their glasses touched with a clear ting in the summer air.

After they'd drunk the toast, Kurt set his glass down. "You know, tomorrow is going to be a big day for you."

Margo settled her glass next to his and sat down on the low railing, looking up at him. Again she felt the butterflies that hadn't abated all day long.

"I hope I can do it, Kurt. Really I do. As much for your sake as for mine."

A frown of concern clouded Kurt's face. "Doubts?"

Margo shrugged. "It's a big responsibility."

Kurt reached a hand for her and she stood up. "Let's go for a walk and give your nerves the evening off."

Kurt guided her to the steps at the edge of the terrace and they descended into the dimness of the gardens she had seen earlier on her tour of the house. The lush tropical foliage was colorfully rich in the moon-tinged darkness, the paths neat and precise. The strong aroma of roses, pine and jasmine drifted around them as they strolled along the banks of man-made ponds and crossed plank bridges over miniature streams.

From somewhere on the hill, only a few hundred yards away, Margo could hear the slightly muffled sounds of a party. The sound of brash music came faintly from the direction of a mansion with all its lights blazing. From this distance, she could see the silhouettes of party-goers on the great house's terrace. Over there, Margo mused, perhaps someone was giving one of the fabled Hollywood bashes.

As she watched the cavorting figures, Kurt reached for her hand in the dim light, and a lightning bolt of feeling jolted up her arm to her heart, surprising her. The skin of his hand was taut and warm, the fingers wrapped casually around her own. She sensed the strength in his hands, a power that she knew came from his agile body.

"Is Cinderella dreaming of going to the ball?" he asked.

They slowed to a stop as Margo turned to him. "Just a little Beverly Hills eavesdropping. Someone seems to be having quite a party up there."

Kurt looked past her at the scene far up the hill and nodded. "That's Lyla's place."

"Lyla?"

"Lyla Webster," he informed her, bringing his attention back to her.

Margo's eyes widened with excitement. "Lyla Webster? You mean *Summertime Rhapsody*—1947—directed by Gordon Barrett—Lyla Webster? She's one of my all-time favorite actresses." She turned her eyes back to the hillside and its Hollywood glitter as Kurt slipped his strong arms around her. They felt comforting. "How I'd love to go to a party like that," she said dreamily.

"You'll be able to give them yourself, someday," he answered softly.

She felt a soft nuzzle of his lips on the side of her head, then the solid plane of his cheek against her blond hair as he turned her to face him and their eyes met in silent communication.

"I wish I had a tenth of the confidence you have in me," she said. Again she felt apprehension, even at such a moment. He was so close, his hands clasping her arms in a caressing hold that was definitely more than businesslike. "Tomorrow morning I'm going to have the anxiety attack to end all anxiety attacks."

"Nonsense," he purred, brushing her exposed shoulder with his warm lips.

The sensation sent a chill down her spine. Despite the tremble that suffused her, she tried to resist the impulses he awakened. As she felt the pounding of her heart increase, her troubled mind reminded her that she shouldn't be letting this happen—this way led to danger.

"I mean it, Kurt. Suppose I'm a flop," she lamented. "Suppose I go in and make a total mess of everything."

"Suppose," he said, putting his index finger over her lips, "you trust me a little." She looked a question. "Margo, I didn't offer you the agreement because I *thought* you could do it. I *know* you can do it. I've seen what you've done with Video Matinee. Your dreams are only a step away from reality."

She turned away, searching the leafy darkness for the courage she lacked. "I'm just afraid."

Kurt's words were soft and smooth. "I can't imagine you being afraid of anything."

"It's the being so close, that's frightening," Margo explained haltingly. "I've always wanted to be able to prove myself, make a name for myself. Then I'd finally be able to have everything I've always wanted— for me *and* the store."

"So?" It was clear from Kurt's puzzled tone that he didn't understand her fears.

"I figured I would work up to my success gradually. I hardly expected to have it handed to me, lock, stock and franchise rights." She turned back to him and their eyes met, hers searching in the dark depths of his for the answer he never quite seemed able to give. "Kurt, why did you offer the deal to me?"

He didn't say anything, just stared tenderly down into her face, his gaze traveling over the halo of her blond hair. Finally, he said, "You have another side— another side than Video Matinee."

"What do you mean?" Margo swallowed.

"I said once that we were two people, not two stores," he said huskily. "You tell me if *you* feel this— or the store does."

He brought his lips down on hers, and Margo melted into his strong supportive arms like wax near a flame. Every inch of skin on her body tingled as his hands moved slowly, sensuously up her back, one finding an exquisitely tender soft spot between her shoulder blades that made her shiver despite the warm night air, the other slipping into her hair to wind a few shimmering blond strands in its caressing fingers.

Margo ached: her body seemed about to burst. Kurt's tender caresses were making her respond in a way that left her confused. She felt the swelling of her breasts, the heightened sensitivity of their tautening peaks. She was so light-headed, she thought the top of her head might just float away. She felt as if every emotion, every fiber of her body, was fighting for release. What was happening to her? Why was she totally powerless to control the responses that Kurt excited in her? These were dangerous emotions.

Margo couldn't control nature and her arms rose to circle him. Kurt's broad shoulders felt massive under her arms, a veritable rock of solid strength. Even through his dinner jacket, she could feel the tenseness of his muscles beneath the fabric and the harsh movement of his hot breath as they kissed.

Kurt's lips left hers, traveling in a delicate trail down the soft line of her neck, and his breath seared her throat, sending a spasm of pleasure down her spine. Margo was enveloped by a mad, turbulent inner desire that reached clear through her, although her mind entreated her to resist, telling her she had been stung before and would only be hurt again.

She had come here on the strength of a promise that exactly this sort of thing would not happen. Now the warning bells that she'd so frequently relied on were tolling a resounding knell, and she forced her mind from its haze of ecstasy to respond to their cautionary call.

Kurt's supple fingers slid from her shoulders and rested against her soft bosom. The brush of one finger along the edge of her swollen breast sent a shock through her that made her emotions skid wildly.

"No," she protested, pushing him away.

Kurt was reluctant to release the prize he seemed to covet. "But why, Margo? Margo..." he breathed huskily, trying to draw her near again.

Margo was more determined this time. "Kurt, no—" She succeeded in breaking his hold and stepped back, turning away. "I don't want this to happen...."

She felt the brush of his palm on her shoulder but didn't move away. "Margo, you want this as much as I do—" he began softly.

Margo closed her eyes and covered her face with her hands. "No I don't," she choked out. Her hands clenched into fists as she turned on him in frustration. "Kurt, you promised me this wouldn't happen. That was our agreement." She knew her hazel eyes must be blazing with anger—both at him and at herself. "I'm here to do a job."

"That's all?" He had retreated silently, respecting the attitude she now presented.

"That's all," she reiterated. "How can I make you understand that? I can't let an involvement between us threaten our work. Anything like this between us isn't right—not now, not here."

A fire of longing was in his dark eyes. "Where, then? And when?"

Margo stared at him in silence. She would have run away at that instant if her principles hadn't kept her rooted to the spot. His words had the sound of an ultimatum, but she refused to be a party to it. She had been afraid something like this would happen, and she'd been right, she just hadn't expected it to happen on the first night.

Where and when, he had challenged her. No—she wouldn't give him the satisfaction of waiting for the moment, crossing the days off on some mental calendar until the time when he could have her without the interference of business. Harsh visions of the oppressive relationship with David Cort swam into her mind. She refused to buckle to that sort of pressure, and he would have to know that immediately.

"This isn't going to work out, Kurt," she said hastily, firmly.

"What do you mean?" A look of puzzled concern crossed his features.

"I think I should leave—go home to Cielito Vista."

"No," he said heavily, grasping her hand. "You can't, Margo."

The clutch of his hand on hers was fire, and she felt an acceleration in the mad beating of her heart. She withdrew her hand. "I think it's best. Out of harm's way and all that. Video Matinee is too important to me to jeopardize its future. I can commute to your store. People commute to Los Angeles all the time—I don't see why I should be any different."

"But you *are* different, Margo," he said, coming closer. His dark eyes showed determination and his jaw was firmly set. Then the look on his face softened. "Don't go, Margo. Please. I just got carried away."

The look that passed between them was full of meaning, and Margo saw a contriteness there that surprised her. She hadn't expected Kurt to back down like that: it was clear that he didn't want her to leave, but why? Was it because her departure would be a blow to that massive ego of his? Or was he truly remorseful for the emotions that he had provoked between them, threatening his promise that she would be safe living with him?

She believed the latter. Kurt took too much pride in his promises. He would rather be drawn and quartered than be accused of breaching his own sense of honor. She stared hard into his eyes.

Expelling a long breath, Margo attempted to bring her pulse back to a more normal rhythm. David's kind of pleading had never worked with her, but Kurt's apology and request held a subtle difference she found impossible to discount. He was right. There was something between them—something she couldn't deny. After a long pause, she said slowly, "All right, I'll stay."

Visible tension drained from Kurt, and his hand found hers in the dimness. Somehow the warm grip seemed reassuring this time, instead of emotionally dangerous.

"You won't regret it, Margo. I promise you that."

Margo couldn't stand the intensity in his dark eyes, and she averted her gaze to the terrace among the trees. "Maybe we should go back to the house," she said softly. "It's getting late. And I'm getting chilly."

Kurt whipped off his dinner jacket and slipped it around her shoulders. The black silk lining was comfortingly warm from the heat of his body, quickly dissipating the chill she'd felt. He pulled the front edges of the jacket together to make sure she was snug and comfortable inside.

Their bodies were close at that moment—dangerously close, again.... But dark memories provided Margo with the courage to turn away and head for the moonlit terrace.

Chapter Eight

Kurt pulled his white Mercedes into the parking lot beside the garishly painted orange building and killed the engine. The size of the Hot Circuit Video store on Hollywood Boulevard was intimidating. The mammoth rectangular building was easily four times the size of Video Matinee, but Margo realized she had made her bed and must now lie in it.

The Hollywood Boulevard outlet was their starting point because Kurt's other outlets had so far evidenced no real effects of mismanagement. They had both agreed it best to start with the worst and nip a possible domino process in the bud.

Margo's stomach knotted when she saw the enormous neon sign with the store's name and logo. The windows were covered with obviously expensive promotional posters and studio stand-ups. Even the store's twenty-five parking spaces made her stomach flutter.

"I only have six...." she muttered with an envious glance at the fully occupied lot.

"Hmm?" Kurt was there beside her.

"Nothing," she said, shaking her head. "I was just admiring your parking lot."

He shrugged as they waited for a red Camaro to ease past them in search of a spot. "It's just a parking lot, as parking lots go."

"I know—but I'm easily impressed."

They started across the pavement to the two wide plate glass doors. "We'll do just as you planned," he said, slipping on a tweed sport coat he'd pulled from the back seat of the car. "We'll go in as a nice, unobtrusive couple and see what sort of reaction we get out of them."

"You're sure they don't know we're coming?" Margo asked.

"They don't even know what I look like," he replied with a laugh, "and I'm the boss."

"Demerit number one," Margo pointed out, unamused. "Try to be visible—if not to your customers, at least to your employees."

The moment Kurt opened the glass door of Hot Circuit Video for her, Margo was assaulted by the blast of air-conditioning, harsh lights and ear-shattering electric guitar. The cacophony stunned her for a second, but then she entered without hesitation. The store tour was starting just as she'd expected. She hadn't had a chance to see Kurt's reaction to this dinning barrage of music and lights, but she could imagine it.

Her fears of the night before, despite Kurt's reassurances to the contrary, were renewed as she wandered over to check out a deteriorating cardboard display. She had expected the worst and had tried to be prepared for it, but the doubts still lingered in her stomach.

The place was definitely disorganized: returned movies sat in voluminous piles awaiting check in and blank tape racks were practically empty with no likelihood of being refilled in the near future. As a couple wandered past her, deeply engrossed in the store's catalog Margo heard the man grumble that he still couldn't find a certain title. She suddenly wondered just how big a mouthful she'd bitten off. This was definitely going to be a difficult one to chew.

Get your bearings first, Margo, she told herself, casting a casual look around the store's interior. Try to see what sort of traffic patterns there are and how well everything is displayed. Can things be found easily? she wondered, resurrecting points she remembered from her merchandising classes in college. What about employees? Are they visible?

A quick glance around told her she was alone. Kurt had disappeared but she could pick him out heading down a side aisle toward a badly hand-lettered sign that stated rudely Rewind Tapes—Or We Charge You.

There was a scattering of people in the six aisles that ran lengthwise down the store, most of them wearing fatigue pants or torn sweatshirts. She was able to pick out a few in some variation of conventional dress; she hoped they were the sales staff.

That hope was dashed—it was impossible to tell the employees from the customers. Maybe they were *all* employees—or all customers. Margo gave a wide berth to a young man whose orange-tinted hair stood up stiffly in all directions, but he turned to her.

"Help you?" he fairly screamed. He must be used to talking when the music was at this volume. A Hot Circuit Video name tag pinned on his designer shirt identified him as Josh.

"Where are your new releases?" Margo shouted back. Apparently it wasn't loud enough, because he looked at her as if she were from outer space. Now, the guitar solo was blaring out again and he was moving his body in time to the tooth-jarring music in a rhythmic gyration she found slightly obscene.

"New releases!" she screamed as loudly as she could. He finally heard her—the whole store heard her. The song had ended as she opened her mouth and it was too late to hold back her shout.

"Jeez, lady." The young man shook his head, giving her a disparaging look. "You don't need to scream—just ask. New releases are down that way," he said, gesturing in the right direction.

"Thanks," Margo replied, and started for the section he'd indicated.

Then she headed toward the back of the store to find Kurt. From large speakers in the four corners of the shop, a new composition raucously blasted her eardrums. The walls, up to the ceiling, were plastered haphazardly with movie posters. Each overlapped the next in utter confusion, creating a hodgepodge of color in a desert of impersonal sterility. Although the poster decorations were a nice touch, simple enough that she should have thought of it for her own store, they'd gone overboard with quantity, she thought ruefully.

A left turn at the end of the aisle brought her to the children's section. Examining a few titles, she noticed the familiar Disney selections and regular Saturday morning fare, but her eyes opened in surprise when she began to encounter horror movies among the cartoons. A couple of ghost stories wouldn't have been too bad, but her searching eyes picked out more and more dubious movies among the tales of Tom Sawyer and Huckleberry Finn. It was enough to make Winnie the Pooh turn over in his grave, she thought.

A soft touch on her arm made her start and she looked up to see Kurt at her elbow.

"Oh," she said. There was no need to whisper for the volume of the stereo rendered normal conversation inaudible to anyone over two feet away. "It's just you. Thank God someone in here dresses as if he's from Earth. What happened to you?"

He did not seem amused. He glanced away, trying not to look as if he were discussing the place with her. "I went to check on the office. You've been busy, I assume?"

She nodded. "Take a look at this," she commented, reaching out and pulling into view an empty videocassette box with an axe-wielding madman decapitating a nurse on the cover. "When was the last time you saw Bugs Bunny and Porky the Pig in league with a homicidal maniac?"

"My God..." he breathed. He turned abruptly and spied a dark-haired girl two aisles over, returning movie boxes to the shelf. "Miss?" he asked. She didn't move. "Miss?" He raised his voice.

Margo nudged him. "You'll have to do better than that. Remember, you're competing with Ace Deaftone and his Earbusters," she said, indicating with her thumb the mammoth speaker up in one corner of the store.

Kurt cupped his hands on either side of his mouth. "Hey!"

His deep, booming voice could have been heard above a nuclear blast, thought Margo, surprised at its ferocity. It served its purpose: the girl turned in their direction. Kurt and Margo came around the end of the aisle and caught up with her as the noise from the speakers died away.

"Can I help you?"

"What's with the horror movies in the kid's section?"

Kurt actually sounds civil, Margo thought. She'd watched an unfamiliar glint enter his eye at seeing *Dumbo* rubbing elbows with *Dead End Massacre*. She had interpreted it as anger—something she had never seen him display. If she had judged that reaction correctly, he was showing an amazing amount of self-control.

The girl's name tag identified her as Lisa. She shrugged unconcernedly. "We just put the movies everybody asks for together, you know. The kids don't want any of this *Cinderella* stuff—they ask for *Night of the Ax* or *Blade Ripper*. Stuff like that."

The girl stowed the last two boxes on the shoulder-high shelves without checking to see they were in the right order, then headed for the front desk, with Kurt following. Margo trailed him, but not before noticing that both movie boxes Lisa had put on the shelf belonged in two separate sections.

Lisa stopped to check a clipboard of figures. Beside her was another young man, this one with blond hair. He wore faded blue jeans and an expensive polo shirt. His nose was firmly planted in a similar clipboard, and he never looked up.

"Come on," Kurt said brusquely, taking her by the arm and steering her in the direction of the rear of the store. "I'll show you where the *real* fun begins."

He opened the door to a small office and showed her in. Inside was a metal shelving unit overflowing with Hot Circuit data, a desk covered with masses of paper and a computer terminal. Kurt flipped on the overhead lights and closed the door.

Margo moved toward the stacks of paper on the desk. The size of the piles was intimidating, but her natural sense of neatness made her fingers itch to tidy the room up at once.

"Going into the paper business?" she commented.

Kurt's expression wasn't amused. "What you're seeing is the aftermath of a big mistake. Take a seat," he said, gesturing to the office chair at the desk and turning to the overflowing shelves.

Margo seated herself gingerly, examining the hodgepodge on the overburdened desk and noting a pile of receipts here, food-stained bills there. Forget tidying, she told herself, I'll just hose the place down and start fresh. Kurt turned from the wall unit with a small sheaf of papers in his hand.

"You might find this interesting," he said, proffering the sheets for her inspection.

She accepted them and began to flip through them. They were inventory sheets with notations as to stock status. A proliferation of red checks looked suspicious, and she was astonished to realize the marked titles were missing movies from the rental stock.

She looked up at him. "Theft?"

"'Misdirected stock' is the way Mike put it," Kurt said sarcastically. "Titles got rented out and no one followed up on them. They're still floating around out there, for all I know. Don't ask how we'll get them back."

Margo swallowed. He had just put the ball into her court. "Well, I can see one thing I'll have to get on right away," she commented. "I'll need a complete list of the people these movies were rented to."

Kurt gestured to the huge mass of paperwork in the shelf unit. "Be my guest. And before you get started on that, I think something else is more important."

He reached around her and brought up the screen on the computer terminal. After a few keypunches, he had the daily receipts in view. He showed her how to scroll the information, and she began to scan the figures, looking for errors.

Her eyes widened, and she gave a low whistle. "You have overages and shortages here that would give the calmest man in the world ulcers."

"Sometimes I wonder if those kids out there know how to count money," he fumed, a dark cast in his usually bright eyes. "I'm tempted to go out there right now and fire every last one of them."

"It isn't their fault, Kurt," Margo said firmly and quickly. "This was all Mike's responsibility. He should have seen that the work was being done, and that the overs and shorts in the daily cash flow were accounted for. I'll lay you ten-to-one odds that none of those kids out there were ever taught how to count out change."

Kurt shrugged sullenly. "All I know is, it's a mess."

Margo turned back to the terminal. "Mess is an understatement. Catastrophe would be more accurate." She looked through a few more figures. "If you're having this sort of problem with the daily receipts, what state are the accounts payable in?"

She found a sheaf of bills pushed under her nose.

"I took care of most of these as soon as I found out the place was in trouble. Some, though, I don't know what to do with. I have statements for merchandise that I've never seen."

Margo looked at the bills with annoyance, her mind already making a list of problem areas: counter help, store atmosphere, daily cash tracking, inventory control; and now shipping and receiving. She had the feeling that this was going to be like starting a store from scratch.

"How are the other stores faring in relation to this?" she asked.

Kurt tapped the computer keyboard a few more times and brought up a store-by-store accounting of his empire. This, Margo thought, looked encouraging.

"Well, it doesn't look as if the harm has spread too far," she said confidently. "Just a couple of the stores are beginning to show irregularities. I think, though, that we can nip it in the bud."

"It's going to be a hard disease to cure," Kurt said blackly.

"But it *can* be cured," she stressed.

"I'm right behind you, Dr. Shepard."

They exchanged a look—his of hope, hers of assurance. In that instant, Margo realized that their business deal wasn't as one-sided as she had thought. There was definitely more to their agreement than making her dream come true.

Hot Circuit Video desperately needed help. She remembered his claims that her creativity and fresh blood would revitalize Hot Circuit Video and realized what he had actually been doing was making a des-

perate plea for help in bringing this Frankenstein's
monster under control. It was clear that while he was
offering her the chance to survive the growing competition, she would also be saving his own chain from
a disaster.

Suddenly, the fact was driven home to her that they
were on the same footing, technically.

"There's a lot of work to do here, Kurt," she said
honestly. "My six weeks are going to be full to overflowing."

"I'm here to help."

"And I'll need it. I think the first step would be to
have a meeting with the staff at the earliest possible
moment."

Kurt made to head out the office door. "No sooner
said than done...."

"Not now," she said, stopping his departure. "Tomorrow morning, before the store opens. It'll give me
time to get some notes together."

He nodded.

"I guess that's all I can do for now. I'd like to stay
here for a little while and try to make sense out of
some of this."

"Be my guest."

Margo shook her head at the nightmare of paperwork surrounding her. "I just hope I haven't bitten off
more than I can chew."

"Don't worry about that," Kurt said with forceful
reassurance. "I'll be here all the time. You don't need
to make a move without me."

"Kurt, I don't need to be guided around by the
hand...."

He sat on the edge of the overflowing desk. "No,
but you need someone to help you blast your way out

of this cave-in. I intend to be here, chipping away alongside you."

"But—"

"No buts," he said with finality, heading for the door and opening it. Halfway out, he leaned back in the door. "We're in this thing together."

After he closed the door, Margo turned back to the computer screen, the knot in her stomach becoming tighter as she had the disturbing feeling that dealing with the store wouldn't be nearly as difficult as dealing with Kurt.

Chapter Nine

Kurt issued a command and, the next day, the staff of the Hot Circuit Video store on Hollywood Boulevard assembled one hour prior to opening. Margo stood with Kurt at the front desk, aware of the grumbling of the employees about the inconvenience of reporting to work early. Yet, the transformation in the store's atmosphere was amazing.

It looked the same as the day before when she and Kurt had infiltrated its rock-music-blasting interior. But the absence of shrieking guitars, and customers who looked like the audience at a rock concert, made a tremendous difference. At last people could hear themselves think.

Margo tensed as the four employees filed in, looking subdued. Their employer had called a special staff meeting to address attitudes and store policy, and they knew that meant trouble.

The situation was playing havoc with Margo's nervous system. Just the silent confrontation between Kurt and his employees was intimidating. The atmosphere at the store yesterday had caused her to stand back a little and review her working relationship with Kurt. It had been hard enough to keep him from firing every last employee in the store; Margo knew it would be even harder to keep his forceful, commanding personality under control. She was here to do a job—and that didn't include wrangling with Kurt. To hide the nervousness she felt, she pretended to study the clipboard of notes she'd drawn up last night, alone in her room.

"Okay," she heard Kurt's gruff voice announce, "I think we're ready to begin."

Discontent radiated from the four employees. Danny, the blond manager, shot a wary glance at Kurt and then at Margo, tightening her nerves another turn, while Lisa, who didn't have her inventory clipboard to hide behind this morning, seemed apprehensive.

All attention was focused on Kurt. at the front counter. "I'm not going to explain why you're all here this morning," he said, leveling his gaze at each of the teenagers in turn. "I think you know why. There are a couple of things you'd better know before we go any further: one—as the owner of this store, I won't tolerate the impression I got of this place yesterday. I can only imagine how legitimate customers feel."

Margo stole a look at the small band of employees and noted that they all had the same caught-in-the-act expression. Dealing with them could easily prove to be a chore, she thought nervously.

"Two—" Kurt continued, "there are going to be some drastic changes around here, starting now. You will adhere to the new rules or you won't be working for Hot Circuit Video. Is that clear?''

Four heads nodded silently. As Kurt slid Margo a look, she felt adrenaline pump through her. This was it, she thought, he's laid down the terms, now it's up to me to explain them.

Kurt returned his attention to his employees. ''Starting today, you will have a new member on your team: Ms. Margo Shepard.''

As he indicated her, all eyes turned to her with a mixture of interest and apprehension, and Margo tightened her grip on her clipboard of notes, suddenly empathizing with Lisa and her protective grasp of her inventory sheets the day before. But outwardly, she was able to greet them with a brisk businesslike inclining of the head.

''Ms. Shepard will be here every day—overseeing the running of the store, studying areas that need attention and implementing any changes she sees fit. If you have any questions about how to handle something during the next few weeks, go to her. She has the authority to make any decisions that need to be made, and I have full confidence in her ability to deal with any problems that might come up.''

Margo and Kurt traded looks. His was a small injection of support, but enough to allow the taut spring inside her to ease slightly. Before she knew it, Kurt had turned the floor over to her and stepped away, leaning on a display case and watching the scene intently.

Margo cleared her throat. Mentally, she crossed all her fingers for luck and began.

After greeting them and expressing the hope that they could all get along, she began to outline her battle plan. She knew none of the items on her list would be met with applause—more likely with great resistance—but she was here to do a job, and Kurt had already spelled out the consequences: you either do it my way or you don't do it here.

Margo checked her notes. "First," she said, using her best business voice, "is employee mode of dress. Beginning tomorrow morning, Hot Circuit Video will have a dress code: all male employees will be required to wear dress slacks, a dress shirt of some sort and a tie." She saw looks of disappointment spreading on the faces of Danny and his assistant, Josh. Before she could become too agitated, she went on.

"Female employees will be required to wear a skirt or dress pants and a conservative blouse. No torn tank tops, no fishnet pullovers and no bare midriffs," she emphasized with a guarded look at the two females on the staff. Obviously their peculiar sense of fashion was offended. Lisa cast a mournful look at her expensive bag dress, and the other girl, whom Margo and Kurt had missed yesterday, was in abject grief. Her name tag identified her as Dawn, and the black kohl around her eyes, her inky stockings and her skintight imitation leather miniskirt made her look absurdly older than her eighteen years.

As her agenda continued, Margo found herself becoming more relaxed. Reassuring glances from Kurt were never far away, but she found herself resorting to his authoritative presence less and less as she described the immediate changes she intended to make.

Hairstyles would be conservative—their colors likewise. Employee attitudes needed to be refocused: rather than customers being regarded nuisances, they were to be treated with respect and courtesy. She reminded them that the money customers spent in the store was the source of their paychecks. Her list went on and on as she outlined procedural changes and new policies.

A major test of wills came with the announcement that rock music would no longer be played in the store. There was strong verbal opposition, but Kurt stepped in firmly and silenced the dissent before Margo could respond decisively.

"But it'll be like a tomb in here," wailed raven-haired Dawn.

"You're here to work, not listen to music," Kurt stated dogmatically.

Danny spoke up defiantly. "All the other stores play it."

Kurt's expression showed that he was becoming irritated. "We aren't going to be like other stores. Isn't that what Ms. Shepard has been trying to tell you?"

Margo could become irritated, too, and she intervened. "Music is all right," she conceded. "But you have to remember, this isn't a record store. You aren't selling the music you're playing." She flipped up a few pages and pulled one out. "I have here a list of music that can be played—at acceptable levels," she pointed out. She handed the sheet around, to dubious looks. "Soundtracks," she explained. "After all, this is a video store. If any music is played, it should relate to the merchandise you're trying to sell—or, in this case, rent."

This decision was accepted with grumbles, but accepted just the same. Margo checked her watch: ten to ten; the store would have to open in a few minutes and she needed to let the kids do their respective jobs. She concluded with a reiteration that by cooperating they could make the changes she suggested easier for them all.

As the four teenagers rose and dispersed throughout the store to perform their opening rituals, Kurt sauntered over to her. He had a grin on his face that only added to the anxiety that had developed in her minutes earlier.

Now that the initial meeting was over, she felt a flood of tension released from her body and could afford to let off some steam. "What are you smiling at?" she asked with an edge in her voice.

"At you. You did a great job. I think they believed every word you said."

She felt relieved, and his words of encouragement made coming down from her businesslike soapbox easier. "Thank you. I think I got through to them."

"I knew one of us would," he said, his expression becoming serious. "It just took a firm hand—"

She had to say something to dispel the feeling coiled up inside her. "I understand why you did it," she began, hoping to soften the blow, "but I didn't appreciate your comments on the rock music."

A puzzled frown crossed his features. "What are you talking about? I was just backing you up."

"Kurt," she said quietly, but firmly, "you weren't backing me up, you were defending me. If those kids think that I can't handle a simple disagreement like that without your intervention, then I haven't got the authority you told them I have."

The look in his eyes showed that he didn't fully understand her reasoning. "I'm not going to let those kids run roughshod over you."

Her hazel eyes blazed. "And neither am I. Kurt, you said you had confidence in me. Then show it."

He caught her arm as she turned away toward the front counter, and a spark passed between them. "Margo, I have every confidence in the world in you, but there's no way I'm going to stand around and watch a bunch of smart-alecky kids question your authority."

Margo felt herself bristling like a cat. "If you have to interfere in everything, the orders I give will mean nothing. You hired me to do a job. Let me do it."

Margo broke away at that moment and headed for the front counter to speak with Danny, the manager. Her heated emotions were making her tremble. She hadn't expected Kurt to be so domineering and protective of her. Foreboding visions of David Cort and his patronizing attitudes toward her floated clearly before her eyes. As she pushed the thought away, refusing to allow her mind to complete the picture, she tried to tell herself Kurt wasn't like David.

But, she realized, she had never been on a business level with him. The sudden thought occurred to her that she might have been misled by his overwhelming ability to make her heart beat faster and her nerves tingle. Maybe it was asking too much that the easy camaraderie they shared on the personal level would show itself in the workplace as well.

They were both headstrong, both independent. She didn't want to think about the two of them meeting head-on in a truly substantial argument. Kurt, she knew, would be forceful and determined to have his own way.

But so would I, she thought with satisfaction. So would I.

Startled, Margo looked up from the notes spread before her on the desk in her sitting room and drew in her breath. She'd been so absorbed in the mechanics of putting together a draft for an employees' manual that she hadn't heard Kurt enter the room.

"You frightened me," she confessed. With one look, she took in his casual outfit of tan slacks and royal blue cotton shirt. The buttons of the shirt were undone just enough for her to see the dark curls that spread underneath it. She looked away quickly.

"I didn't mean to," he said earnestly. He came forward and leaned against a chair. "You know, this job you're doing doesn't involve any overtime."

Margo blinked up at him, puzzled. It was hard to focus after concentrating for so long on her own precise handwriting.

Kurt pointed to the gold wristwatch on his arm. "It happens to be after midnight."

"After midnight?" Margo turned in her chair and looked at the tall arched window. All she saw was inky blackness outside. "Do you mean I've been at this for nearly four hours?"

"More like six," Kurt commented. He reached and shut the spiral notebook in which she'd been working. "Come on—you need a rest. You won't do me any good if you wear yourself out."

She raked her fingers through her blond hair, pulling the strands back from her face and gently massaging her weary temples. A sigh of tired satisfaction escaped her lips.

"I haven't heard any complaints in the past two weeks. Let's just say you're getting your money's worth from me," she said, pushing back her chair and standing up. Stretching to unwind and relax, she realized how tense she'd been from bending over the desk.

"I'm getting a lot of employee for the money," he said, his chocolate eyes chastising her, "but precious little houseguest. I hardly ever get to see you."

The weariness left Margo in an instant, and she was quick with a reply. "I thought we had a deal: you'd stay in your part of the house and I'd stay in mine."

"You forget," he said, his dark eyes sparkling with amusement, "that *all* parts of the house are mine. It's my house."

"You know what I mean," Margo insisted.

"Yes, I know what you mean." His tone was rueful. "But that doesn't mean you can't come out of your cubbyhole once in a while. Why don't you come downstairs with me and have a drink or something before turning in."

The idea was appealing. She definitely could use something—anything—to drink. Besides, it was late and she was tired: a drink would ease sleep's approach. "Okay," she agreed. "Only, the strongest thing I want is a cup of tea."

Fifteen minutes later he escorted her outside to the terrace, and she settled into a red chaise lounge with the promised mug of steaming tea in hand. Los Angeles was spread before them, alive even at this late hour with thousands of lights. The sky was cloudless and she could see the bright spray of stars overhead in the mild summer air.

Kurt straddled a lounge chair, facing her, and sipped his tea. "You should slow down a little, you know."

Margo turned her relaxed attention to him and gave a tired smile. "Don't lecture a workaholic. It just makes them work more."

"You're doing wonderful work," he said quietly. "You're pulling all the loose ends together just like I knew you would."

His praise made Margo feel good. She had been giving of herself one hundred and ten percent and was gratified that her diligence and hard work had begun to pay off. Most of all, she told herself, she was proving to Kurt what a good businesswoman she could be when given the chance.

"I appreciate that," she said simply. "But I have you to thank for having enough confidence in me to give me the job."

His dark eyes were sparkling. "I've always had confidence in you. You're one hell of a woman, Margo. A man could lose his head over a woman like you."

Margo felt tense. He had introduced the forbidden subject again and it made her nerves tingle. Since the near indiscretion in the moonlit garden her first night, he had maintained a respectful distance and she admired him for it—admired him because she could see in his eyes and in a thousand other ways that she attracted him like a powerful magnet. An arrested hand movement, a quickly averted eye . . . She looked down to the cooling cup of tea in her hand, an apparently innocent late-night refreshment.

Her fear that the unseen housekeeper, Mrs. Post, was merely a ruse to entice her into coming here had been dispelled. Meals were prepared, beds were made, housework was done—these things hadn't happened by themselves. Invisible the woman might be, but the constant reassurance of her presence—if you could call it that—made Margo feel better. All so proper, all so correct . . . but all so tense.

She was aware of the sexual spell Kurt seemed to be under when around her, because she felt the same way about him. She'd sat awake too many nights lately, wrestling with her feelings, and just thinking about him was a volatile proposition. He'd lectured her about spending too much time with her work, but what other refuge did she have? It was the only thing she could do to keep her mind off him.

With alarming regularity she had to keep reminding herself just what she was doing here. Despite Kurt's passionate appeal, she tried hard to maintain the hold on her dream. As she'd told him all along, Video Matinee came first. But why did she feel this way? What inner something caused her concentration on business to flee after two seconds alone with Kurt?

Margo shook her head, bringing her attention back to Kurt and the present. "What did you say? I'm sorry—"

Kurt smiled indulgently. She focused on the tiny crinkles at the corners of his eyes that added even more character to his unique features.

"I said I'm glad you decided to be my consultant. I don't think I could have found a prettier one if I'd tried."

Alert now, Margo swallowed. Was she being too complacent about their romantic silence? Had it been nothing more than the proverbial calm before the storm?

"Kurt—" she began firmly.

"Now, come on," he entreated her. "I've been good. No advances, no worries."

"I don't know what you're leading up to...." Her tone was cautious.

"I happen to be leading up to flattery," he explained, putting his mug on a wrought-iron table at his elbow. "I don't know of any laws against telling you you're a beautiful woman. A lot of successful women are beautiful, but none have your mixture of intelligence and wit."

Margo felt a nervous warmth in her veins. She was ready to quickly quash any romantic feelings he aroused in her, but his approach confused her.

"Nothing's going to happen between us," she said with less conviction than she felt, putting her mug aside.

"Something has already," he informed her. His eyes didn't hold any amusement.

It was impossible to tear her gaze away from the message in his shadowed eyes. Deep inside, she felt the detonation of emotions she'd tried to suppress. She felt the warmth of his hand as he gently brushed away a lock of hair from her cheek. His attraction was overwhelming and she'd resisted it for so long.

She cupped her hand over the hand he rested lovingly at the base of her neck amid her blond tresses. His face was close to hers now, close enough for her to feel his warm, gentle breath.

Kurt's words were soft in the warm night air. "You can't tell me there's nothing between us. Not when two people are as perfect for one another as we are. You've heard the term *two of a kind....*"

Margo smiled, thinking the same thing as Kurt's hand moved slowly and easily through her hair, his caress easing the resistance in her body. As a tantalizing wave of feeling flowed through her, she closed her eyes in pleasure, and melted at his touch, realizing how much she had missed it, had longed for it.

His lips met hers and her last resistance dissolved. He pulled their bodies close together in a tight, possessive embrace, his hand in her hair, guiding her lips to his. His tongue gently invaded her mouth, and he tasted her sweetness with a groan of pleasure that rumbled from deep inside him, as his chest pressed against her swelling breasts, shooting thrilling sparks of desire through her. His body was hot and his blazing skin seemed to sear her flesh. He drew her over on top of him as they fell back on his lounge chair.

Instinctively, every fiber of her being blended with his, feeling his bold passion as he lay beneath her, his muscles rigid with desire. He passed a firm, caressing hand over the small of her back, sure and strong, pressing the most vital parts of their bodies together as if they could occupy the same space, and she clung to his massive shoulders like a lifeline, feeling the taut muscles beneath his shirt.

Her fingers, overcome by a sensual power she couldn't control, traced a path through his silky hair, and she drew her hand down the plane of his neck, feeling the strong pulse of desire flowing there. In amazement, she realized it echoed her own furious heartbeat, which was pounding desperately.

"I can't apologize," Kurt said in a low breath. "I know we agreed—"

She placed her fingers to his lips to stop his words, but he paid them no attention.

"You've done something to me.... You're like no woman I've ever known."

Margo pressed her cheek to his solid shoulder. "You said yourself that we're two of a kind."

She felt a wonderful completeness at being in Kurt's arms, but something stronger pricked at her mind.

Kurt's vital masculine presence and firm, deft caresses went against everything she stood for—and were everything she tried to avoid. Always, she resisted strong and dominating men, ran away from them or faced them down. But with Kurt Lawrence her subconscious seemed to take a stand opposing her common sense.

What was she doing? Kurt had maneuvered her into the precise situation she had warned herself against: loving kisses, moonlit nights, sweet nothings—manipulation, she reminded herself in a jolt of reality. She recognized the signs. And she knew what these things led up to, what performance she was expected to give.

Kurt brushed aside the collar of her blouse, his hot lips sliding to the smoothness of her shoulder. She writhed as his touch traced a delectable, wet path toward the hollow in her neck, lower to her... Although her skin ached with warmth at his tender touch, a screaming voice inside her called a halt to her compliance. It was as if past hurts had thrown a mammoth roadblock across her emotions.

Kurt was aware immediately of her sudden and unexpected resistance.

"What's wrong, darling?" he asked in whispered concern.

Margo sat up, feeling strangely cold in the warm summer air, surprised at the sticky perspiration that made her clothing suddenly uncomfortable. She couldn't speak. Her mind was a maze of confusion.

Kurt placed a tender hand on her shoulder and Margo stood up quickly, crossing the terrace to stare, without seeing, into the black canyon below. He followed her.

"Is something the matter, Margo?"

"I don't know. No...yes..." Tears of frustration welled in Margo's eyes. She'd let this happen, let Kurt Lawrence engineer the last few moments and had been powerless to stop him. She wanted to believe that the torturous feelings invading her heart were caused by her aversion to male manipulation and her sudden inability to resist it. It couldn't be anything else, she tried to convince herself. It couldn't....

Kurt's warm arm circled her waist and she tensed at the feelings she couldn't bring under control.

"Do you know what you mean to me?" Kurt began soothingly.

Margo's senses were on the edge. She had to escape.

"No..." she said pleadingly, stepping out of his hold. She turned to look at him and saw concern and caring in his eyes. As her heart swelled in response to his deep, magical gaze, she fought the urge with enormous willpower.

She couldn't look at his face any longer, not when her mind superimposed memories of David on Kurt's clean, dashing features. She ran from the moonlit terrace into the safety of the house.

Another week's work on the store went by quickly.

Adhering desperately to her appointed task, Margo walked a wide, wary circle around Kurt. Home life wasn't the same after their brief encounter. She was jumpy and tense, replaying the scene over and over in her mind. None of these reruns brought her any sense of security; they only made her question the outcome more than ever.

Meals consisted of polite conversation, both of them careful to avoid the subject in the forefront of their minds, and Margo felt guilty and uncomfortable. Throwing herself into Hot Circuit's problems, she tried to dispel in her own mind the possibility that she had already knuckled under to Kurt's magnetism and dynamic self-assurance.

Slowly but surely, she was solving Hot Circuit Video's problems. The mountains of paperwork were scaled to the last sheet. A full inventory of stock had been completed, and once she had set the kids to tracking errant movies they had recovered a sizable number. Cash handling had been streamlined, overages and shortages became exceptions, rather than the norm, and shipping and receiving was coming along nicely.

Margo had drawn up a working plan for rearranging the interior of the store and the plan was taking shape. The long rows of video racks stretching the length of the store were separated into distinct units placed at intervals and different angles throughout the spacious floor area. This, she explained to the staff, allowed a variety of merchandising positions and avoided one section of movies slipping over into another. The teenage employees admitted the new arrangement looked more attractive.

She was satisfied with the rapport she'd slowly built with the staff; once the kids decided she wasn't there to make a nuisance of herself, but to make their job easier and more enjoyable, they were open to her ideas. The only problem had been Dawn.

The girl had never quite recovered from the absence of rock music in the store and was vocal about it to anyone who would listen. Things simply were not working out with her, no matter how hard Margo tried to make her a member of the team, and when she adamantly refused to cooperate, Kurt fired her—tersely, angrily.

As Dawn fled from the store, Margo was astonished by the ferocity with which Kurt had handled the girl's dismissal. He had been short and to the point with no room for plea bargaining, and the incident produced a rage in Margo that surprised even her.

After Dawn left in tears, Kurt retreated to the private office in the back of the store to close out the girl's time sheets and make up her final paycheck. As he looked up from the computer terminal to check a time card, Margo confronted him.

She stepped into the office and closed the door. "Kurt—" she began, trying hard to keep the fury out of her voice.

Kurt's expression was hard. "She had to go, Margo. You knew that, I knew that and the kids on the floor knew that." He punctuated his words by viciously punching a few buttons on the computer keyboard and brought up the payroll screen.

"Why didn't you let me handle it?"

"I was fed up," he said shortly, and she could see the angry flex of a muscle in his jaw. "Dawn was not going to stay here and tell me what she was going to do and how she was going to work. I'll be damned if an employee of mine is going to defy me and go against all the orders and plans you've made—"

Margo released her anger quietly. "Then wasn't that up to me? If she wasn't following my orders, it was my job to dismiss her. Isn't that what you hired me for?" It rankled that Kurt would snatch the authority from her. When he didn't answer, she went on. "Kurt, you never even worked with the girl. You only come to the store three days a week, and I work with her every day. I would have done it myself, but—''

The silent look that passed between them was electric, but there was no malice in it. She never felt any anger directed at her during these skirmishes—only a mute plea for understanding. But something in his look this time was different and suddenly she knew what it was as she felt her blood pressure rise.

''You don't think I would have done it,'' she accused. ''You think I'm a pushover for those kids out there. That they can get away with anything because I'm a marshmallow.''

''I never said that,'' he said, turning his attention to the computer screen.

''But you're thinking it, aren't you? If that's what you think, then why don't you fire *me*?''

''Stop talking nonsense.''

Margo tossed her head in fury. ''I'm not talking nonsense. And I'm not a marshmallow, either. I would have fired Dawn when—''

Kurt didn't look up, but began inserting amounts into the screen showing Dawn's file. ''That's not good enough. The situation had gone on for too long.''

''Do you show up when I'm working just to make my job more difficult?'' she asked hotly.

''I just like to check on your progress,'' he said, eyes intent on the screen.

''To see if I'm doing my job?'' she asked with fire in her eyes. How she wished she could make him look at her.

Her silent wish was granted: the eyes he turned to her were so deeply brown, now, they looked black. ''I happen to like what you're doing for the store—I like seeing you make a diamond out of a lump of coal. If you think my coming to the store is a disruption of your authority, maybe I shouldn't come at all.''

The retort on her lips died at once. She hadn't intended the argument to deteriorate this way; the last thing she wanted him to think was that he had no right to be in his own store while she was working.

"Kurt, please," she said, dropping all pretense at anger, "you know that isn't what I want any more than you do. I'm trying to do something great for Hot Circuit and it's difficult if I have to worry about— well, about not measuring up."

The hard look in Kurt's eyes disappeared immediately and concern flooded his features. "Margo, I don't want you to think you're doing a bad job. I want to be with you to see the turnaround. Things have fallen by the wayside as my businesses got too big." He reached for her hands and held them. "It's exciting to see you mine the potential here."

Their eyes locked and a communication, a silent understanding, passed between them. Margo could feel the tension in Kurt's warm hands. This was his first physical contact with her since the night on the terrace, and dangerous sensations in the pit of her stomach, anxious longings that threatened to bring back old hurts, began to creep through her every fiber. She suddenly looked away, withdrawing her hands.

"I—have a surprise for you," he said quickly, too quickly. He slipped behind the computer console and pulled out his jacket, and from the inside breast pocket, withdrew a long white envelope that he held out to her.

Margo accepted the envelope and slit the seal with her fingernail, drawing out the contents: an expensive deckle-edged white card. She flipped it open and smiled as she read it.

"An invitation," she said, at once flooded with excitement, "to the Annual Classic Films Convention— Oh, Kurt, I've always wanted to go. How did you know?"

"Aside from the fact that you wander through life as if you live in an MGM musical," he smiled, "you might call it a lucky guess."

Margo reread the invitation. "On the *Queen Mary*— Oh, God, art deco paradise. Wait'll I phone and tell Jo."

"You're supposed to come as your favorite movie star," Kurt supplied.

"I always wanted to be Marlene Dietrich or Hedy Lamarr," Margo decided. "Who are you going to be?"

Kurt shrugged. "I don't know yet. The convention isn't for three weeks," he added. He was silent for a moment, and she felt uncomfortable in the searching look he gave her. "I said I was sorry, Margo. I am."

She realized suddenly that his words meant more than they seemed to: he wasn't just apologizing for overriding her authority; he was apologizing for that night on the terrace. He'd recognized the fear in her, a fear she couldn't tell him about, and he blamed himself for her reaction.

A lump rose in Margo's throat. Perhaps it was the words she needed—but couldn't bring herself—to say, or an emotion she was too afraid to show. She couldn't possibly explain to Kurt what made her tense up in his arms. She stared blankly at his probing eyes, then turned quickly and left the office before she began to cry.

Chapter Ten

Kurt called Margo away from her breakfast on the terrace. As she entered his study through French doors, she saw Kurt turn from the large white enamel and chrome desk, the telephone receiver in his hand.

"It's Jo," he said.

Margo's pulse quickened with expectancy. She hadn't heard from her manager in nearly two weeks and was anxious for news about how Video Matinee was faring in her absence. As she took the receiver, Kurt told her quietly he'd wait for her on the terrace and finish his customary morning coffee.

As soon as Kurt was out of the room, Margo put the instrument to her ear. "Jo? Jo, how are you? How's it going?"

Her manager's familiar wry voice came on the line. "I'm fine. Have you made the Fortune 500 yet?"

"Not quite," Margo laughed. "What's up?"

Jo paused meaningfully on the other end of the line. "I want to break this gently...."

"Do I have to sit down?" Margo asked apprehensively.

"It wouldn't hurt," Jo advised.

Margo turned to a futuristic art deco chair and thumped into it. "Okay, I'm sitting down."

Another pause. Margo knew it must be serious if Jo punctuated her conversation with so many silent stretches.

"Somebody bought the lot on Faulkner Place."

Jo's voice sounded tinny and impersonal, or maybe the news just made it seem that way. Margo was stunned.

The voice on the line went on. "I just found out yesterday. The place has been graded and a foundation's been poured. The way I figure it, the lot was bought about two weeks ago."

"No!" Margo's exclamation was full of disappointment as the vision of her dream store came to mind, and she watched as some faceless contractor erased it with a bulldozer. "Do you know what's going on the lot?" she asked.

"I'm not sure. Bobbie said he heard it was going to be another JiffyBurger outlet. It's the perfect spot for one."

"It is *not* the perfect place for one," Margo said with exasperation. "My *store* is the perfect thing to put there. They sold it out from under me. Jo—this is terrible. What are we going to do?"

"Margo, it isn't the end of the world. There are other lots all over town. We just took too much time picking up the option on it, I suppose. We can find another spot."

Margo was sullen. "I suppose you're right."

She hung up, unhappy and thoughtful.

When she returned to the terrace, Kurt picked up on her mood immediately. "Bad news?"

She stood in the doorway, a picture of resignation. "My lot's been sold," she said simply. Kurt didn't say anything. He didn't need to. He couldn't be expected to know what that lot meant to her.

She crossed to the terrace railing, not seeing the gardens spread below, the canyon beyond that or the city of Los Angeles moving like a giant machine. She felt Kurt's hands touch her shoulders cautiously and her first instinct was to shy away, but instead she leaned back, allowing herself to seek comfort in his strong presence. Kurt gingerly encircled her with his arms, trying to restore a slight sense of security. She could tell he felt as if he were walking on eggs.

"Margo, there's nothing you can do about it now," Kurt said logically, but his voice was tender. "If the lot's sold, the lot's sold."

She nodded. He was right. Jo was right. "But everything was going so well." She clenched her hand and regarded the tight fist. "I nearly had my dream right in my hand—so close I could taste it." She relaxed the hand, leaning further into his embrace as if his solidity was enough to supply her with the self-confidence she lacked at the moment.

"Just because the lot's been sold doesn't mean you don't have a dream. There are plenty of other lots."

"I know," Margo confessed sadly. "And it's stupid of me to feel this way. I guess I'd just wanted it for so long that I felt I already owned it. Boy, does the bank have a way of bringing you down to earth."

"I know you, Margo. You won't let a little thing like this bog you down. You've dealt with worse things than losing a vacant lot." He smiled. "You've even dealt with me."

Despite herself, Margo smiled weakly. *But I haven't dealt with you*, she thought almost desperately. *I don't know how. That's part of my problem.* Somewhere in the back of her mind was the absurd thought that losing her lot was some sort of divine retribution for allowing her reserve to drop where Kurt was concerned. If she hadn't begun to give in, would the lot still be up for grabs? She discarded this fanciful notion.

Her troubled thoughts were trying to sort out too many things, and the lot was only a small part of it. There were other places in Cielito Vista to build her store. It just meant her steamroller of a dream had been halted for a while. She wasn't out of the running yet.

Her feelings for Kurt were something else. When he touched her, he did something to her, something she couldn't explain. It was an alien feeling, different from what she'd felt for David. In many ways, Kurt was so much *like* David: forceful, dynamic, manipulative, maybe even more so than her ex-fiancé. But there was something in Kurt that wouldn't let her condemn those qualities, the same qualities that had sent her running to escape David's clutches.

And for some reason, it all didn't seem to matter to Margo. Right now she was just grateful for his presence and support in a moment of defeat. If nothing else, that practically earned him the exclusive right to hold her.

"Thanks for being here," she said, resting her head on his shoulder.

"That's what I do best," he reassured. "You know what I think you need?" he said quickly, straightening up and holding her at arm's length.

"What?"

"To get back to work," he advised. "Take your mind off the lot."

Margo shrugged. "Maybe you're right...."

He turned her to face him. "Of course I'm right. You can tear yourself up inside over this, but the best thing for you is to dig right back in." His eyes held a curious expression, and there was a concern there that spoke some silent language. "Your six weeks are almost over."

Margo nodded agreement to his logic, but she still felt disturbed and upset, without a tangible reason. Was she just tense and tired, now that her job as consultant was drawing to a close?

"I suppose we should start for the store," she said with a look at her wristwatch. "It's nearly ten."

Kurt reached for a last sip of coffee from his cup on the wrought-iron table. "I have a little more bad news for you this morning. I'm afraid I won't be able to go to the store with you today."

Margo turned a puzzled look on him. "Why?"

"You forget," he said, fixing her with a reproachful eye, "I have two other businesses to run. Unless you want to have to come in and revamp those, too, I'd better start paying a little attention to them."

"Well, I suppose you really have to...." She was surprised to find she couldn't keep a disappointed tone out of her voice.

"I'm going to be pretty busy for a week or so. I've let things go for as long as I can," he said. He checked his own watch. "I'm going to be late." He gave her a deeply understanding look. "It's all right, Margo. You can do it by yourself."

She stared at him for a second before he smiled and bent to kiss her, then he was gone.

Margo stood alone on the terrace for a full five minutes after his departure, feeling that things had moved too fast for her this morning. Something wasn't right. Kurt had acted—how? As if he'd *wanted* to get away from her. What have I done? she asked herself. Then the thought occurred to her: what *haven't* I done? Their entire relationship had been a series of false starts, with her always running and hiding. When he had given her the tickets to the Classic Films Convention, she had been closer to showing her affection for Kurt than at any other time, but then she had fled.

Kurt knew—he wasn't a fool. She was handicapped by her emotions, afraid to give either herself or Kurt a chance.

The dull ache in her heart was proof that the spirit was there but the flesh unwilling. But what would be the result? Had she made Kurt as frightened of her as she was of him?

Kurt's visits to the store had slowed gradually since he'd fired Dawn. Now it was rare if he stopped in twice a week and he hadn't been in this week at all. Margo saw him when she returned to the house every night, but dinner conversations simply weren't the same as having him there around the clock. Invariably, he was gone by the time she came down for her toast-and-coffee breakfast.

She had continued to do her job, though, pushing now toward the completion of the six-week trial period. At the end of that test period, she would have her dream in her hands—vacant lot or no vacant lot.

The thought that she had lost out to someone else on the prime location still made her blood pressure rise, but she had taken Jo's words to heart: she'd find another—and better—site. Cielito Vista was a burgeoning town on the new California Gold Coast and its growth would be tremendous; she put her trust in the economic forecasts.

Margo cupped her hand to her mouth and called onto the floor. "Lisa, when you get a chance, come and tell me how this looks."

She heard Lisa's hearty, "As soon as I can, Ms. Shepard."

As Margo stapled a wide sheet of black construction paper to the back wall of the display case in the front window of the store, her thoughts dwelt on Kurt's absence from Hot Circuit. Was this how the problems with the business had started in the first place? Kurt had said his overwhelming duties with Bonnie Lee Pastries and his late father's construction firm had robbed him of the time to keep track of the video store's progress.

If that was the case, she thought as she secured the bottom of the construction paper, then it would happen again if he wasn't careful.

She stepped back to admire her handiwork but didn't really see it.

"Admit it, Margo," she scolded herself harshly under her breath. "You think he's grown complacent about Hot Circuit Video with you in charge."

Rather than considering that possibility to her credit—that he trusted her enough with the franchise that he was leaving it entirely to her—she could only see the negative side. Had Hot Circuit Video, and Margo herself, become just another cog in the Lawrence, Limited, corporate machinery? She didn't want to believe that, but Kurt's continued absence tended to fuel such thoughts. She didn't even want to think how much her skittish emotions had contributed to the current state of affairs. If she dwelt on it, she would only end up making herself sad.

She began to stick a red cardboard border to the black background with masking tape, liking the effect. Pulling the step ladder closer, she climbed it and reached up to apply the top strip of the border.

Only a few days ago she had suddenly realized that the long awaited Classic Movies Convention aboard the *Queen Mary* was this weekend. Tomorrow. She had been indecisive about her costume from the moment Kurt had given her the invitation, but she had finally decided. She reminded herself that she needed to stop by the costume shop on Sunset on the way home and pick up the disguise she had chosen.

No matter what frame of mind she might be in, the convention was something that deserved her full and wholehearted attention. She might never have the chance to go again, and she wanted to make the event special. The outfit she had chosen was a treat. She refused to let her worries diminish the anticipation of wearing it.

Since the convention coincided with the end of her six weeks, she knew her work here was almost finished. This would be the last weekend she spent at his house, the last day in the store and the last time she would be working with the kids. She was heartsick now that the day to pack up and move on had sprung up so soon. She really liked the kids now: they had all done such a good job of helping her turn the store around.

Climbing down from the ladder, she cast an appraising eye around the transformed store. With true satisfaction, her eyes scanned the attractive arrangement of shelf units and the chrome-framed movie posters. She was rightly proud of the promotional displays that she had labored over with creative fervor. The big black speakers at the four corners of the store poured forth muted instrumentals from a movie musical.

It had all turned around beautifully. Cash was accounted for, stock likewise; the counters were being covered, movies were being put away without a backlog. Her work, she was glad to see, had halted any domino effect, and the other outlets that had begun to show signs of cracking were whole again, thanks to her expertise.

Danny was behind the counter, helping a middle-aged customer bag a small pile of films. She smiled, realizing that, compared to six weeks ago, it was a phenomenon that anyone over twenty could be in the store without going out of his or her mind. Lisa was helping a couple on the floor, showing them the new releases. Margo thought the girl looked attractive in her white skirt and royal-blue blouse. A lot of the credit is theirs, too, she reminded herself.

She turned back to the display window, pulling out an adventure movie poster that showed Burt Reynolds fighting a snake and fending off the amorous advances of some actress at the same time. She stapled this at an angle, managing to pinch her thumb.

With a muffled oath, she sucked on her finger to dull the ebbing throb, her thoughts turning to her own store while she waited for the pain to subside.

She'd become fiercely protective of Video Matinee in the last couple of weeks—even more so than usual. The dark thought that Kurt might consider his own store, and her in particular, as just another facet of his booming corporate empire made her even more eager to finish her job. As long as she felt this way, she didn't believe her own Video Matinee was safe. If she remained in danger of being taken over by Kurt Lawrence, then her store was in as much danger as she was.

She was startled by the appearance of Lisa's naturally copper-colored head around the edge of the display case.

"How's it going, Ms. Shepard?"

Margo took a second to push her gloomy thoughts into the back of her mind and remember that she had called for Lisa to come take a look. "It's coming along great. Come on up and see for yourself."

Margo helped the girl up the two-foot rise and into the window. Lisa stepped back and surveyed the three-quarters finished display with a satisfied eye.

"Great!" was her pronouncement. "The movie was terrible, but the window's fantastic." She giggled.

Margo smiled. "You're here to push the movies," she reminded her jokingly, "not pan them."

"You didn't see the movie," Lisa said in the same spirit. She looked the window over again, then said, "You know, Ms. Shepard, you've done a lot of good things in this store. I don't know about the other kids, but I want to thank you for what you did for me."

Gratitude filled Margo's heart and she smiled her thanks for the compliment. "It wasn't really me, Lisa. All I did was remind you kids of what you already had in you. Believe me, you put in a lot of effort, going along with my changes."

"Well, you worked pretty darned hard. The way we hear it, you saved our jobs by saving the store. As a matter of fact," the copper-headed girl said seriously, "you really look tired. Have you been getting enough sleep?"

Margo laughed at the comment, thinking that the girl couldn't know what kept her awake at night. Agonizing about her own store; worrying that she would finally succumb to Kurt Lawrence's charms, to his domineering personality...

Margo nodded. "Sleepless nights are right," she nodded, not willing to go any further. "I'm just a notorious party animal," she joked.

A skeptical look came into Lisa's eyes. "If you're a party animal, then I'm Princess Diana." Her look became serious again. "You're worried about something, aren't you?"

Margo nodded again. It couldn't hurt to admit that much.

"I hope it isn't about leaving us," the girl was quick to say. "You don't need to lose any sleep over us, Ms. Shepard. Now that you've shown us what to do, we'll be all right."

Margo turned to staple another poster to the backing. "You kids are only a part of it, Lisa. People worry about a lot of things and I just worry about more of them than most."

"I'd say you're worried about Mr. Lawrence."

Margo froze and slowly turned back to the girl. "What did you say?"

Lisa looked as if she knew she might have said too much, but she continued. "You really like Mr. Lawrence a lot, don't you? You do," she said, not waiting for an answer, "I can tell. I've seen you look at him the way I look at the guys in rock groups."

Margo was staggered. Out of the mouths of babes, she thought in stunned silence. "You must be imagining things, Lisa," she said, trying to give the shocking remark less weight.

"Oh, no," the teenager said firmly, "it's serious, all right. Don't think I'm trying to be a busybody or anything, Ms. Shepard, because I'm not. I'm just telling you what I've seen."

Margo was almost afraid to ask. "What have you seen?"

Lisa swallowed. "Well, I've never seen Mr. Lawrence look at you when I didn't think that he was madly in—"

"I get the idea," Margo said hastily, putting down the stapler and climbing out of the display window. Lisa followed.

"Ms. Shepard, he really goes for you," Lisa said earnestly. "I think we're talking serious relationship—like on *The Love Boat* or even *Dynasty*."

Margo couldn't believe her ears. If all this was so evident to Lisa, then all the kids must know it. And for heaven's sake, who else knew it? She felt herself blush and grow warm all the way from her Adidas to the top of her head. A strange tide of emotions flooded through her. Was it because she knew it, too—and had known it all along? She'd been in love with Kurt Lawrence for weeks now. She made her subconscious confess it. It was true. And she'd tried to run away from it.

"Has Mr. Lawrence ever said anything to you about it?" Margo asked, not caring now if Lisa saw how interested she was.

The girl looked horrified. "Oh, no, Ms. Shepard. He's never breathed a word. And don't tell him I told you all this. I like working here now—I don't want to lose my job."

Margo patted the teenager reassuringly on the shoulder. "I promise you I won't say a word. And no one's going to get fired."

Lisa relaxed visibly. "Oh, wow! You had me going there for a minute. As long as you know, then, it won't come as a shock."

Margo's senses were alert. "A shock? About what?"

Lisa was startled by the older woman's intense reaction. "About the cake, Ms. Shepard."

"Cake...?"

"In the back room. Mr. Lawrence came in and delivered it when you went to do the window. He said it was for you and not to let you know until after he was gone."

Margo left Lisa's words far behind as she raced for the office and flung the door open. On the now-immaculate oak desk was a bakery box, the top propped open. She came around the desk to see for herself what Lisa thought would be so shocking.

A luscious round cake rose up out of the box. On its top was a miniature version of her dream store with an icing-covered marquee. Across the marquee was written in appropriately art deco lettering: "One hell of a job, baby. Thanks to you, our dreams are coming true. My Love, K.C."

Chapter Eleven

Kurt was there when she arrived home from the store, cake in hand.

She was contrite: her thank-you couldn't possibly compensate for the negative thoughts she'd harbored about his corporation and his supposed attitude toward her.

"I don't need a thank-you," he said warmly, pulling her close to him with a relieved, winning smile. "I should be thanking you—a million times over."

Margo turned in his embrace so that her slim back was pressed against his solid body. As his arms tightened around her, she felt the security of a comforting cocoon wrap her—body and mind. She had been wrong about Kurt Lawrence. He was a deeply sensitive man, and she felt guilty that he had been as much a victim of her past hurts as she had.

"I'm sorry, Kurt," she said quietly.

"Sorry? For what?" he asked softly, his mouth close to her ear. His lips nipped tenderly at her ear, sending a pleasing glow through her. "If anyone is sorry, it's me. I'm sorry I didn't find you sooner."

Margo smiled. "Especially for the store's sake."

"For my sake," he corrected. He turned her around to face him and the intensity and honesty of his gaze brought a lump to her throat. "Let's start over again."

"Start over?" she said, puzzled.

He nodded. "Hi, my name is Kurt Lawrence," he smiled.

Margo laid her cheek on the solid firmness of his shoulder. Forget the skirmishes. Forget the past. The future is what counts, she told herself. A tear of relief and joy began to course down her cheek.

"Pleased to meet you, Mr. Lawrence," she said softly. "My name is Margo Shepard...."

Margo felt the delicious brush of warm lips through the muslin and organdy that covered her shoulder as Kurt came up behind her in her cabin on the *Queen Mary*.

"God, you look positively gorgeous. This was definitely worth the wait," he breathed and turned her to him.

The maneuver wasn't easy. Margo's yards of carefully pinned black and white floor-length skirt were hard to deal with. At first, the rakish upsweep of her feather-laden picture hat and her black wig felt unsteady, but the effect soon passed. She managed to keep her delicate balance with the matching parasol, propping it against the edge of the cabin's chair like a buttress on a top-heavy cathedral. She sighed in exasperation—the buttons on the white kid gloves were coming undone again.

Kurt looked marvelously swarthy. A white, bloused shirt opened down his chest, revealing its dark curly expanse against his healthy tan. High-waisted, tight black pants tucked into calf-high buccaneer boots gave him a dashing air and outlined every muscle in his legs. On his usually clean-shaven face was a false mustache—pencil-thin, but completely in keeping with Kurt's character role. It only served to make him more dashing.

"Errol Flynn at your service," Kurt announced, sweeping her a chivalrous bow.

Margo smiled. "I don't know what you think, but Errol Flynn and Eliza Dolittle make a pretty weird pair."

"I'd say it's perfect," he said, coming close and putting his arm around her beribboned waist. "You're *my* fair lady, and you deserve better than Henry Higgins." He studied her face for a second. "You know, I don't think I could ever get used to you as a brunette."

Margo laughed. "Don't worry. It's all special effects."

And what special effects, she reminded herself. She had meticulously rehearsed the proper application of the makeup and wig. Her disguise as Eliza Dolittle from *My Fair Lady* was a labyrinth of petticoats and buttons.

It had been almost impossible to keep the gown a secret from Kurt. He had pestered her about it since she'd brought it home the day before, sealed in a tight plastic covering. On the drive from Beverly Hills to the *Queen Mary*'s permanent berth in Long Beach, he had tried valiantly to break down the clandestine barrier she had thrown up around her outfit.

As they stood now in her half of their two-cabin suite, he kissed her, long and deliciously, his lips meeting hers hungrily. As his tongue parted her lips, and she tasted the freshness of his mouth, the false mustache on his upper lip crinkled and tickled. As he bent over her, pushing her head back, she gave a throaty laugh of pleasure. Kurt's lips turned her into a live wire, and she felt the current charging through her.

He turned her head, placing kisses in a line down her cheek and fanning a flame in her. Her skin tingled with energy—his energy—and she felt herself melting willingly into his possessive arms...and realized suddenly that her hat was slipping off. She protested, but he held her firmly, indulging himself and exciting her with soft nips at her neck.

"I'm falling apart," she breathed.

"Good," he said through the tiny kisses he was giving her, "I've always wanted to be the downfall of a woman."

Margo smiled. "I mean my costume." Brought back to reality, he released his hold on her waist and she steadied herself again with the parasol. "Eliza Dolittle never got anything like that from Henry Higgins," she said breathlessly.

Kurt winked at her, an evil smile crossing his mustached lips. "You bet your sweet swashbuckler, she didn't."

They made their grand entrance into the *Queen Mary*'s Main Salon in style. Margo only had to stoop slightly to get the hat through the double, beveled glass doors to the palatial, three-story high ballroom. All heads turned when she entered on Kurt's arm, and she could feel everyone's eyes following the restrained, courtly gait she had to affect in the elaborate period gown. Her role was instantly recognizable to the crowds of other movie star impersonators around them.

"Ah, Miss Dolittle," a pudgy Captain Bligh greeted her, bowing to bestow a lifeless peck on the back of her begloved hand. "So glad you were able to join us."

"Please let me introduce Mr. Errol Flynn, Captain." The words rolled off her tongue with practiced ease. She squeezed Kurt's arm affectionately as she effected the introduction. "Professor Higgins was unable to come."

Kurt and "Bligh" exchanged a good-natured handshake.

"Seen any good mutinies lately, Captain?" Kurt asked the rotund skipper, grinning slyly beneath his dark mustache.

"None," Bligh assured him with confidence. "I've just signed on a man I know will keep such nonsense under control. Name's Christian—Fletcher Christian."

Margo wanted to laugh at the obvious humor of their exchange, but strained to keep her stately flower-girl-turned-lady composure. Instead, as Kurt led her away, she favored the captain with a dazzling smile. "I'd watch him, anyway, Captain. Who knows what may happen on the high seas?"

Kurt propelled her deeper into the crowd, and she turned to face him, dropping out of character for only a moment.

"Kurt, this is wonderful," she said with enjoyment. "It's like going to classic movie heaven."

He slipped his arm from its formal hold of hers and dropped his hand to her waist. "It's as if the Chinese Theater had exploded," he laughed.

Margo couldn't take her eyes off the bizarre conglomeration of pseudo-stars surrounding them. "More like a Hollywood premiere gone berserk."

The atmosphere and people were marvelous, a dream come true. She had heard about the Classic Films Convention many times over the years and had always longed to go to it. Now that she was actually here, she felt right at home. This sort of movie madness was lifeblood to her, and she was glad to see that Kurt was drinking it in as well. With her dashing Errol Flynn on her arm, this was one Eliza Dolittle who really could dance all night.

Margo had been too excited for much conversation en route to the *Queen Mary*. She had barely managed to deflect Kurt's curiosity over her tightly wrapped costume in the back seat. Once on board, she couldn't have asked for more. Since the first moment, she had been in a movie dreamland. At every turn, faced with more and more delightful episodes involving would-be movie stars, Margo pressed Kurt's strong hand warmly to let her appreciation for this experience travel silently but firmly to him. By the tender hand squeezes she received in return, she knew he was happiest when she was happy. She felt like a schoolgirl at the senior prom with the class hunk. But it was more—so much more.

The rest of the day passed in a whirlwind of music, laughter and chance encounters with imitation movie stars. A woman dressed in a canary-yellow cabaret outfit and a headdress of fruit coaxed her into letting her prized Dolittle composure down enough to join in a rousing Carmen Miranda samba out to the Promenade Deck.

It was nearly eight o'clock when Margo and Kurt returned to their two-cabin suite three decks below to change for dinner, and Margo was grateful to be free of her costume at last. The day's frenzied activities had made the outfit unbearably warm.

Margo changed into her planned dinner costume, a floor-length, white satin gown—simple, elegant, and revealing. She styled her own shiny blond hair into the appropriate Carole Lombard waves. Kurt had dispensed with Errol Flynn and reappeared in meticulously tailored evening clothes. With his hair slicked back, he affected his best William Powell imitation. Dinner would be right out of *My Man Godfrey*.

Dinner was a quietly romantic affair in the shipboard restaurant, Sir Winston's, on the uppermost deck of the *Queen Mary*'s huge superstructure. A meal of crêpes and prime rib was accompanied by Moet and Chandon champagne. During the meal, they were treated to the mellow music of a small four-piece combo.

Margo was dazed by every second of it, and the day began to catch up with her. When her eyelids began to droop, she suggested a walk around the boat deck before they turned in.

The night air was cool and invigorating. Evening mist hung low over the water in such a way that it gave the wonderful impression that the *Queen* was actually at sea instead of tied up permanently at her Long Beach pier. The smell of the sea was fresh and crisp, and a light breeze rolled gently across the deck as they walked without any hurry under the great white lifeboats hanging from their davits.

Margo stopped at the railing and leaned against it, sighing euphorically. "This is so beautiful. You'd think the only thing out there was miles and miles of ocean," she said, nodding toward the starboard side, "instead of the Long Beach Convention Center."

She trembled in the breeze, and Kurt slipped behind her, encircling her with his arms. His lips nibbled gently at the back of her neck.

"More surprises tomorrow, pet. Just you wait."

"Kurt," she said, "what happens now?"

He brought his head around to look at her. "With what?"

She searched his dark eyes in the dim light from the muted deck lamps. "With us," she said conclusively. She let herself be cradled closer to him, and her heart warmed when his embrace tightened.

He seemed to pick his words carefully. "What do you want to happen?"

Margo's lower lips trembled. She fought the tears in her eyes.

"Why tears?" he asked tenderly.

"I've been so afraid," she managed.

Kurt frowned with soft concern. "Afraid of what? Of me?"

She looked away from him and back out at the ocean mist. She settled back into his arms. "I've wanted to let go, Kurt. Really I have."

"I understand...."

She shook her head slowly. "I don't think you do. There's something—a bond between us...."

"You're so special to me." His words were soft and gentle, but matter-of-fact. "No other woman in my whole life has ever affected me the way you have. Everything and everyone pales next to you. Fettuccine will never be the same—I'll always want it dumped in my lap. Just eating it will seem pretty dull from now on."

Margo laughed softly, despite herself. Ironic, she thought, that I'm usually the one tossing out the jokes. But Kurt didn't remain playful for long.

"I love you," he breathed onto her neck warmly, sending a rippling tide of sensation through her. "I've loved you from the beginning—when you first jumped in my lap and I stole a kiss from you."

Margo reveled in his sweet words, feeling his strong body next to hers. She had wanted to hear him say those words for so long. Had wanted to say them herself, but . . .

"I realized a long time ago that loving you would be difficult," he said.

"Difficult?" Her voice sounded muffled.

"I've questioned myself many times. I've wanted to ask if you cared for me a thousand times. But there was always something. I always felt a wall between us."

She made to turn around, but he held her firmly in his arms, facing out to sea. She tried to speak, but Kurt got there first.

"It was David, wasn't it?" he asked.

So he knows, Margo thought. She wasn't sure if she felt relief or anguish but she nodded silently.

"I don't know what he did to make you react the way you have," Kurt said determinedly, "but if I ever meet him again, I'm going to get together a tar-and-feather party."

Margo finally turned around and pressed her fingers to his lips. "Don't talk about David. Not tonight. Not ever."

The thickening mist closed around them, their eyes locked in a timeless understanding. "You always run away from me. This is one time you're going to stay put." He guided her lips to his, and their fusion was electric.

Kurt's tongue parted Margo's lips, and tasted them luxuriously, as a moan escaped from her throat. This was one glorious moment when Margo didn't want to resist him, and she proved it by arching toward him, their bodies fitting together like interlocking pieces of an intricate puzzle.

She gave no thought to heeding warnings, because those cautions were no longer there. The relief of not having to worry about giving away her heart made her giddy, and if it had been possible, she would have screamed with joy. No longer did she have to resist her natural urges. The fear within her that had entreated her to escape his embrace was gone, and finally she could give of herself totally and know how real love felt. There was an ecstasy, a completeness, in holding Kurt in her arms and being encircled by his.

Kurt's lips ran over her mist-dewed face, nibbling hungrily at her eyelids and stroking the shell of her ear, while the powerful rigidity of his body betrayed the passion he felt for her. She could feel the awesome masculine force he held in check, and her own body reacted in an alien, but magnificently instinctive way.

The sensations he awakened were impossible to suppress, and she made no effort to do so, revealing her compliance with a breathless sound meant only for his ears.

"You—only you," Kurt sighed into her ear. "Forever and ever."

The relief flooding through her made her mind a blur. She was in the arms of the man she loved and who loved her; that was all that mattered. The whirlwind of the day cast a wonderful glow on her mind. Kurt's lips on her throat, the fairy-soft mist, the plaintive call of a distant foghorn—these she would remember for an eternity.

Through the open porthole, Margo was awakened by the moan of the twin air horns attached to the forward funnel of the *Queen Mary*. She shook off the last traces of the night's deep sleep as the vibration caused by the horns' call shook the bed with a barely perceptible movement. Coming out of a haze of dreams, she smiled at the memory of last night. She hadn't had to resist Kurt anymore—she could be his and not worry. His good-night kiss at the door that connected their cabins had been long and delicious, and she had enjoyed every single emotion swirling in her head.

She rolled over, expecting to see the cabin's honey-colored woodwork glowing in the early morning sunshine. Instead, she saw off-white. It took a moment for her eyes to focus, but when they did, she was astonished.

On the bulkhead over the side of the bed hung a blueprint. The draftsman's work was sleek and precise, detailing a building of considerable size. Puzzled, she studied the drawing carefully, and her eyes widened. A kid's corner. A catalog center. Lobby kiosks. A side elevation showed a marquee over the front door.

Her first thought was that she was still asleep and her dreams were playing tricks on her. Then she heard a sound from the bathroom connecting her cabin and Kurt's.

"Kurt?" she called tentatively. She propped herself on one elbow and rubbed her eyes.

Kurt popped his head around the bathroom door. His chin was half covered in white lather and his gray-flecked black hair was a disaster area of just-out-of-bed tangles. He grinned broadly. "The sea siren stirs," he said.

Margo made a silent, confused gesture toward the blueprint over her head.

Kurt smiled again. "How do you like it?"

Margo found her voice. "What is it?"

"I thought you knew what your own dream store looked like," he chided, leaning against the door frame. "Awfully forgetful of you."

Margo sighed. This was getting her nowhere. "I can see *what* it is. But why?"

"I promised you more surprises. Well, surprise number one."

Margo looked again at the architectural rendering as an uneasiness spread over her like a thick blanket. "Kurt, there was nothing in our agreement about this," she said apprehensively.

"That's why it's called a surprise," he informed her, stepping back into the bathroom. She heard the sound of water being run in the sink.

She couldn't take her eyes off her suddenly tangible dream—the dream she had strived and worked for for so long. Now, without warning, Kurt had conjured it out of thin air.

A cold feeling that was distinctly disturbing ran through her veins. She began to feel familiar strings pulling her like a marionette. It was one thing, she reasoned, to give her the means of attaining her dream, but it was entirely different when that dream was acquired for her.

She was out of bed in a second, pulling a sheer robe over her nightgown. She stood firmly in the door to the bathroom.

"I want an explanation, Kurt," she said shakily, pointing at the blueprints.

He turned from examining his chin in the mirror and put down his razor. "I'm keeping my promise to you."

Margo gritted her teeth. "What promise?"

"The one I made last night," he said simply, returning to his mirror and razor. "Like I said—'more surprises.'"

"I don't like surprises," Margo stated firmly.

"You'll like mine."

Margo would have thrown something at him if she'd had a handy object within arm's reach. "Kurt, I'm not kidding...."

"And neither am I," he informed her. "We have an appointment at ten-thirty. I'm going to hop into the shower real quick. You'll need to hurry—we don't have much time."

Margo felt lost in an open sea. "An appointment? Where? For what?"

The only answer she got was a wink from Kurt as he closed the bathroom door.

"I wish you would tell me where we're going," Margo said for the umpteenth time. She didn't look at

Kurt. She was too busy studying the Pacific Coast Highway as they headed north along the edge of the ocean.

"I told you," Kurt said, also for the umpteenth time, "It's..."

"...a surprise." They said the words together as if on cue.

Margo lapsed into silence. She didn't like this one bit: if there was one thing she hated more than being manipulated, it was being kept in the dark. A mixture of the two didn't put her in a pleasant mood at all.

She tried to tell herself to go along with it. It was a game. Our relationship began that way, she reasoned. After all, I'm a perfectly wonderful, fun person when I want to be. Get with it, she urged herself.

It wasn't working. There was no way to get into the spirit of things after waking up to find her dream staring at her—tied up neatly and nicely with no effort. Everything had seemed so simple last night. How had it suddenly become so agonizingly complicated again? If only he'd say something!

She chanced a guarded look at him behind the wheel of the white Mercedes. He was dressed for summer in a light, cream-colored suit with burgundy shirt and white tie. It was an attractive effect, she thought, though she was well aware that anything he wore looked good on him. His dark hair ruffled in the breeze from the open window, and he kept his eyes firmly on the road. She could see a slight smile on his lips.

I think he's enjoying this, she fumed, just as he enjoyed telling her what to wear. The white skirt and blouse with red vest and shoes had been his choice. He'd been so adamant about it that she had finally

given in. But as a defiant statement she'd added a
garish orange scarf around her neck. He hadn't asked
for it, she thought rebelliously, but he'd gotten it.

Obviously they were going someplace where she
needed to look civilized. They were headed north.
Ventura? Santa Barbara? Realizing that Cielito Vista
was on the way, she thought wryly: I should make
Kurt stop so I can say hello to Jo in the store.

Suddenly the surrounding landscape became familiar. Maybe she would get her silent wish after all, she
thought as Kurt took the off ramp for Cielito Vista.
Another look in his direction revealed nothing. If all
drivers were this intent on the road, she thought
blackly, there wouldn't be any accidents.

Back in her own hometown, Margo felt a measure
of security, but she was struck by her sense of aliena-
tion, even though she had only been gone a short six
weeks. It's amazing, she thought, how the old place
looks so interesting after you've been gone for a while.
It was a good feeling to regain her bearings after her
absence.

She knew immediately where they were. Kurt made
a wide left turn onto Faulkner Place and sped up,
staying in the right lane, and out of habit, Margo
watched for the ValuMart shopping plaza on the left
side of the road. That sprawling complex with its California Spanish motif always acted as a landmark for
her vacant lot.

No, she had to correct herself sullenly. Not her vacant lot—not anymore. Someone had bought it. Some
jerk had snapped it right out from under her....

Margo's thoughts ground to a halt as she wondered
how long she'd been playing the fool. Things were beginning to fit together, now. The lot purchased, the

blueprints, the secretive drive up the coast. It all added up to...

"There she is," Kurt announced, slowing the car.

As they pulled up to the curb, Margo spied her vacant lot. Only it wasn't vacant now. Someone had been busy—someone she thought she knew really well.

"Surprise number two," Kurt said as he set the parking brake.

Margo didn't even hear him. She was out of the car in a second and standing before the chicken-wire-enclosed building site before he could even turn the car off.

The lot had been graded as smooth as glass and the foundations poured. Clusters of burly workmen were busy at work hammering the redwood frames together on the ground before walking them into place. Some of the framework was up and she could get a general idea of the way the place would eventually look when finished. The sight of her own plans taking shape before her made her want to scream.

She felt Kurt's presence beside her.

"What is this?" Her voice shook with barely controlled rage.

"It looks suspiciously like a dream coming true to me," he replied offhandedly.

Tears stung Margo's eyes. This was the proverbial last straw. This camel's back had finally broken.

"You knew all along," she said bitterly. She turned to face him, her hazel eyes blazing fire. "When Jo called me about the lot being sold—you knew. You'd bought it. You sat there and didn't say anything. You held me in your arms and all along you knew."

Her biting words took Kurt aback. "Margo," he began hastily, "I couldn't tell you. I wanted to surprise you. Darling—"

Margo covered her ears. "Stop! Don't say things like that. I'm not your 'darling' or your 'honey' or—or even your 'poopsie,' for that matter!" She turned away from him, unsure of her next move. Her mind was running at high speed now, turning over recent memories with the velocity of a movie being shown in fast motion.

"Margo, if you'll let me explain..."

She wouldn't let him continue. "No. No, let *me* explain. This is another of your not-so-subtle manipulations, just like your contract, like living at your house, like my coming to work for you: all geared for maximum effect and all with the same goal in mind. Just like—just like..." She had to break off. Her own tears stopped her.

Kurt's voice became hard. "Like who? Like who, Margo?"

He deserved every curse she could hurl at him, but at the moment she was speechless. She remembered all the false starts, all the romantic interludes. She remembered last night, when she had at last been unafraid in his arms. The ache in her heart was too much. At least David hadn't broken it—that had been Kurt's job. Now past images merged with new. He wanted to know who?

"You're no different from David," she spat.

She saw the muscles of his jaw tighten and a steely glint enter his dark eyes. "David is nothing but a loudmouthed oaf," Kurt said through gritted teeth. "Is that your problem? You see me as just another David?"

Margo looked up at him, not frightened by the black expression on his face. "You both find it awfully convenient to manipulate my emotions toward your own ends. You both seem to view me as a possession."

"You have a lot to learn about love," Kurt said firmly. Strangely, the hard cast to his eyes had faded. "David was a caveman, with pretty damned primitive methods. What you mistook for a lover was an idiot in human being's clothing."

An open challenge seemed to exist between them, and Margo took up the gauntlet. "And you're so different? I suppose getting me to stay at your house while I worked on your store was a purely humanitarian gesture."

Kurt sighed and looked away. She would get the truth if it killed him—or her. "Okay, I'll admit you didn't need to stay at my place. But I had to get you away from David. And I needed to put some distance between you and your watchdog, Jo."

Margo leaned back against the hood of the car, crossing her arms. "I'm listening." Her anger had dried her tears, but she sniffed a couple of times for good measure.

"Despite what you think, everything someone does for you doesn't involve manipulation or one-upmanship," he informed her. "Do you think I enjoyed having to tell you that Hot Circuit Video was a mess? Do you think I took pleasure in showing you what a crummy businessman I was?"

Margo swallowed. She shifted on her feet. Another sniff. "Well, no . . ." she said reluctantly.

Before Kurt could say anything else, a burly work-man from the site sauntered up on the other side of the wire mesh fence.

"You all right, miss?" He eyed Kurt suspiciously.

Margo nodded. "I'll let you know if I need any help."

The workman tipped his hard hat and, with a single look back, ambled away to return to his work.

Kurt finally found his voice. "You know, this is a little more difficult than I expected. I had no idea I'd be accused of horrible crimes against you. All I wanted to do was—"

"What are you leading up to?" Margo demanded.

Kurt stopped short. "A proposal," he said pointedly.

Margo's eyes widened. "I've had enough of your proposals. It was one of your *proposals* that got me into this mess in the first place! I'm sorry, Kurt, but you can go peddle your *proposals* to some boob down the block. One who doesn't mind some fast talking or having her dreams bought for her in the hopes of getting a good return on your money."

Kurt was silent for a full minute as Margo's heart shrieked to take back every single word she'd said. Last night, she thought wildly. Oh, God, if only it could be last night! She wouldn't be forced to say these things, wouldn't be forced to believe them.

"I *would* make the same proposal to the boob down the block," he growled matter-of-factly, "only I don't happen to want to marry *that* boob. I want to marry *you*." He stopped short. "Wait a minute. That's not exactly the way I wanted that to come out.... Well, dammit," he said, gesturing heatedly toward the partly-framed structure behind him on the lot, "if you don't recognize a wedding present being built when you see it, then—''

His words sputtered out. They traded indefinable looks for what seemed a very long time. Then, Margo found herself laughing.

She saw Kurt blush for the first time. "You know what I mean."

Once she got started, Margo found it difficult to stop. "Oh, I know what you mean, all right."

"Then quit laughing."

She was able to muffle her mirth, but nothing could hide the wide smile on her face. "That has to be the worst marriage proposal I've ever heard in my life."

Kurt frowned. "Well, give me a break, will you? I've never done it before." He paused, then continued. "What is it you want from me?"

"Kurt, I don't want anything," she stressed. Her smile began to wane. "You just don't understand...."

Pensively, Kurt came closer. Just by his half-checked gestures Margo could tell he was exercising an amazing amount of self-control. "You're the one who doesn't understand. Margo, can't you see that I—''

Margo stiffened. This had the ring of familiarity, an oft-heard line from the past. "If you say 'I want you,' I'll paste you one right here."

He was closer still and she felt her heart beating with jolting intensity. "I don't want you, Margo. 'Want' is a word for people who like to play games—dangerous games with feelings."

Kurt's hand found its way into her hair, and Margo closed her eyes as their special chemistry stirred once again. She felt the tingle of his touch through her whole body. What was wrong with her emotions? Why couldn't she maintain a clear head and an iron resolve against him? She tried to convince herself again that it was Kurt's amazing power to control her, but that excuse seemed dead. It had died last night as they stood on the boat deck of the *Queen Mary*, locked in each other's arms.

"Kurt..." Her voice was unexpectedly breathless.

His words were tender and loving. "Margo, I *need* you. You've made my life complete. I can't imagine existing without you—or you without me."

He was right. Her heart would explode if she continued to deny it. He'd said the magic word, though she hadn't known what it was until that moment. Need. Yes, it was a need, a fulfillment they had together. She had repulsed the feeling for so long, positive that it was only a trap—a whirlpool that would draw her back into a past of hurt feelings and shattered plans.

She couldn't exist without him: she needed his smile, his wry humor, his quizzical right eyebrow. She needed the warmth and oneness they shared when their desires met and melded. She hadn't just become used to him, she had become a part of him, and he a part of her.

A tear rolled down Margo's face to mingle with the lips she suddenly, unexpectedly, pressed to his. Kurt's strong arms encircled her with a warmth that she was relieved to feel again. His touch was a fire that consumed her suspicions, making her his willing partner for the rest of his life—their life.

She slowly opened her eyes and looked up into Kurt's chocolate-brown eyes. The love she found in his shining gaze was enough, for the world around her had ceased to exist.

"Yes," she said softly.

Kurt blinked. It took him a second to catch up with her. "Yes?"

Margo began to smile again. "You really aren't very good at proposals."

The smile that flowed across Kurt's face was wonderful. Before she could say another word, Kurt had swept her up into his arms, one arm supporting her back, the other cradling her knees. He headed through the break in the wire mesh fence around the building site.

"Kurt, what are you doing?"

He trudged across the graded area where the parking lot would be and stood in the framed entrance of her dream store.

"I may have made a mess out of the proposal," he said, his dark eyes twinkling, "but this is one part I'm going to get right if it kills me."

He ceremoniously carried her over the threshold of the structure and set her down on the concrete floor. Around them, work had stopped as dozens of workmen watched this strange performance in the midst of their daily chores, but Margo barely noticed.

Her lips met Kurt's again in a bond she knew would last forever. The builders resumed their work, but the raucous whining and banging of their equipment seemed far away.

To Margo, it was the singing of her heart.

*   *   *   *   *

Take 4 Silhouette Desire novels
and a surprise gift

Then preview 6 brand-new Silhouette Desire novels—delivered to your door as soon as they come off the presses! If you decide to keep them, you pay just $2.24 each*—a 10% saving off the retail price, *with no additional charges for postage and handling!*

Silhouette Desire novels are not for everyone. They are written especially for the woman who wants a more satisfying, more deeply involving reading experience. Silhouette Desire novels take you beyond the others.

Start with 4 Silhouette Desire novels and a surprise gift absolutely FREE. They're yours to keep without obligation. You can always return a shipment and cancel at any time.

Simply fill out and return the coupon today!

* Plus 69¢ postage and handling per shipment in Canada.

Clip and mail to: Silhouette Books

In U.S.:
901 Fuhrmann Blvd.
P.O. Box 1867
Buffalo, NY 14269-1867

In Canada:
P.O. Box 609
Fort Erie, Ontario
L2A 5X3

YES!   Please rush me 4 free Silhouette Desire novels and my free surprise gift. Then send me 6 Silhouette Desire novels to preview each month as soon as they come off the presses. Bill me at the low price of $2.24 each*—a 10% saving off the retail price. There is no minimum number of books I must purchase. I can always return a shipment and cancel at any time. Even if I never buy another book from Silhouette Desire, the 4 free novels and surprise gift are mine to keep forever.

* Plus 69¢ postage and handling per shipment in Canada.

225 BPY BP7F

Name   (please print)

Address   Apt.

City   State/Prov.   Zip/Postal Code

This offer is limited to one order per household and not valid to present subscribers. Price is subject to change.

D-SUB-1D

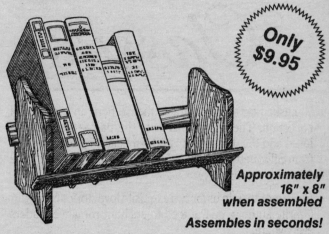

COMING NEXT MONTH

#562 IF YOU LOVE ME—Joan Smith
Lovely maid-of-honor Robyn Halton had the wedding-bell blues. She loved the best man—handsome Sean Blake, her old flame. Always a bridesmaid? Not if Sean could help it!

#563 SOMETHING GOOD—Brenda Trent
Rachel Fentress lived by the rules of simplicity and order. The last thing she needed was a dashing, happy-go-lucky man like Coleman Walker. The trouble was, Rachel's reaction to Cole had her heart eager to break all the rules....

#564 THE SWEETHEART WALTZ—Susan Kalmes
As broad-shouldered Jess Kimball whirled her about the dance floor, Alexandra James nearly forgot her love for the fast-paced city. Jess was one special man, and she wanted to take it slow, but Alexandra couldn't stay in Alaska forever—or could she?

#565 THE MAN OF HER DREAMS—Glenda Sands
Ex-cop Lance Palmer was a hard-boiled realist—hardly the type of hero romance writer Charity Lovejoy usually dreamed up. But collaborating with virile Lance to write a romantic thriller was proving to be a true adventure!

#566 RETURN TO RAINDANCE—Phyllis Halldorson
Eight years ago scandal had driven Carol Murphy from the sleepy town of Raindance, Nebraska—and from the man she loved, Bryce Garrett. But Carol had changed, and now she was back—daring to hope that Bryce could learn to love her again.

#567 SOME KIND OF WONDERFUL—Debbie Macomber
Once upon a time there was a beautiful, sensitive woman named Judy Lovin. Could Judy's love tame the enigmatic, attractive John McFarland—a man who had stunned her senses and captured her heart? Book Two of Debbie Macomber's LEGENDARY LOVERS TRILOGY!

AVAILABLE THIS MONTH:

#556 NEVER LOVE A COWBOY
Rita Rainville

#557 DONOVAN'S MERMAID
Helen R. Myers

#558 A KISS IS STILL A KISS
Colleen Christie

#559 UNDER A DESERT SKY
Arlene James

#560 THE OUTSIDER
Stella Bagwell

#561 WIFE WANTED
Terri Herrington

Silhouette Romance™

Legendary Lovers Trilogy

BY DEBBIE MACOMBER....

ONCE UPON A TIME, in a land not so far away, there lived a girl, Debbie Macomber, who grew up dreaming of castles, white knights and princes on fiery steeds. Her family was an ordinary one with a mother and father and one wicked brother, who sold copies of her diary to all the boys in her junior high class.

One day, when Debbie was only nineteen, a handsome electrician drove by in a shiny black convertible. Now Debbie knew a prince when she saw one, and before long they lived in a two-bedroom cottage surrounded by a white picket fence.

As often happens when a damsel fair meets her prince charming, children followed, and soon the two-bedroom cottage became a four-bedroom castle. The kingdom flourished and prospered, and between soccer games and car pools, ballet classes and clarinet lessons, Debbie thought about love and enchantment and the magic of romance.

One day Debbie said, "What this country needs is a good fairy tale." She remembered how well her diary had sold and she dreamed again of castles, white knights and princes on fiery steeds. And so the stories of Cinderella, Beauty and the Beast, and Snow White were reborn....

Look for Debbie Macomber's *Legendary Lovers* trilogy from Silhouette Romance: *Cindy and the Prince* (January, 1988); *Some Kind of Wonderful* (March, 1988); *Almost Paradise* (May, 1988). Don't miss them!

SRT-1